THE KING'S DAUGHTER

GRACE LIVINGSTON HILL
L I B R A R Y

THE KING'S
DAUGHTER

ISABELLA ALDEN

LIVING BOOKS®
Tyndale House Publishers, Inc.
Wheaton, Illinois

Living Books is a registered trademark of Tyndale House Publishers, Inc.

Scripture quotations are taken from the Holy Bible, King James Version.

Library of Congress Catalog Card Number 94-61525
ISBN 0-8423-3176-X

Printed in the United States of America

99 98 97 96 95
6   5   4   3   2   1

CONTENTS

Welcome vii

Foreword xi

1. Dell's Return Home 1

2. The Young Mistress 10

3. The Letter and the Visitor 19

4. Signing the Pledge 28

5. The Temperance Meeting 36

6. The Drunkard's Home 45

7. The Infant Class 54

8. Finding Recruits for the Temperance Army 64

9. The Tea Party 74

10. Dell's Visitors 85

11. How to Teach Reckless Boys 94

12. The Temperance Dialogue 104

13. A Strange Scene in a Barroom 114

14. A Trip to Boston 123

15. The Review 132

16. Principle or Expediency 140

17. Little Mamie's Death 148

18. Signing the Pledge the Second Time . . . 157

19. The Wedding and the Wine 165

20. The Sad Funeral 174
21. Jim Forbes's Speech 183
22. The Fire 191
23. The Doctors and Their Patient 199
24. The Strange Wedding 207

WELCOME

by Grace Livingston Hill

As long ago as I can remember, there was always a radiant being who was next to my mother and father in my heart, and who seemed to me to be a combination of fairy godmother, heroine, and saint. I thought her the most beautiful, wise, and wonderful person in my world, outside of my home. I treasured her smiles, copied her ways, and listened breathlessly to all she had to say, sitting at her feet worshipfully whenever she was near, ready to run any errand for her, no matter how far.

I measured other people by her principles and opinions, and always felt that her word was final. I am afraid I even corrected my beloved parents sometimes when they failed to state some principle or opinion as she had done.

When she came on a visit, the house seemed glorified because of her presence; while she remained, life was one long holiday; when she went away, it seemed as if a blight had fallen.

She was young, gracious, and very good to be with.

This radiant creature was known to me by the name of Auntie Belle, though my mother and my grandmother called her Isabella! Just like that! Even sharply sometimes when they disagreed with her: *"Isabella!"* I wondered that they dared.

Later I found that others had still other names for her. To the congregation of which her husband was pastor she was known as Mrs. Alden. And there was another world in which she moved and had her being when she went away from us from time to time; or when at certain hours in the day she shut herself within a room that was sacredly known as a study, and wrote for a long time, while we all tried to keep still; and in this other world of hers she was known as Pansy. It was a world that loved and honored her, a world that gave her homage and wrote her letters by the hundreds each week.

As I grew older and learned to read, I devoured her stories chapter by chapter. Even sometimes page by page as they came hot from the typewriter; occasionally stealing in for an instant when she left the study, to snatch the latest page and see what had happened next; or to accost her as her morning's work was done, with: "Oh, have you finished another chapter?"

Often the whole family would crowd around when the word went around that the last chapter of something was finished and going to be read aloud. And now we listened, breathless, as she read and made her characters live before us.

The letters that poured in at every mail were overwhelming. Asking for her autograph and her photograph; begging for pieces of her best dress to sew into patchwork; begging for advice on how to become a great author; begging for advice on every possible subject. And she answered them all!

Sometimes I look back upon her long and busy life, and marvel at what she has accomplished. She was a marvelous housekeeper; knowing every dainty detail of her home to perfection. And a marvelous pastor's wife! The real old-fashioned kind, who made calls with her husband, knew every member intimately, cared for the sick, gathered the young people into her home, and loved them all as if they had been her brothers and sisters. She was beloved, almost adored by all the members. And she was a tender, vigilant, wonderful mother, such a mother as few are privileged to have, giving without stint of her time, her strength, her love, and her companionship. She was a speaker and teacher, too.

All these things she did, and *yet wrote books!* Stories out of real life that struck home and showed us to ourselves as God saw us; and sent us to our knees to talk with him.

And so, in her name I greet you all, and commend this story to you.

Grace Livingston Hill

(This is a condensed version of the foreword Mrs. Hill wrote for her aunt's final book, *An Interrupted Night.*)

FOREWORD

———— ＊✦＊ ————

by Robert Munce,
grandson of Grace Livingston Hill and author of
The Grace Livingston Hill Story

TALES OF ISABELLA ALDEN:
THE NEW YEAR'S ADDRESS THAT
ALMOST WASN'T

Isabella's career as an author started in a modest way and at an early age. As a child she had a short story published in the local paper. The story told how the family clock, which was over a hundred years old, suddenly stopped. The family and the sun overslept, for the sun was using the same clock to wake up by. Without the chime at 6 A.M., the sun didn't know when to get up! Fortunately for the whole world, the father of the family, who was up before dawn, looked at his watch and reset the clock before any real damage was done, thereby averting a world disaster.

Isabella's second attempt as a writer came at age twelve. Again it was for the newspaper. This time it was a truly important assignment. In those days, the 1800s, on New Year's Day the young people who delivered the papers would come to your house, ring the doorbell, and hand you the paper. They would then wish you a most happy New Year and read the Carriers Address to you. This address would then be handed to you, and, as custom demanded, you would wish the carrier a happy New Year and give him a gift of food or money. As you can imagine, this was an important time for the carriers, and the address had to be just right. So they asked Isabella to write their address for them in the form of a poem.

While she feared rhyming was not her greatest talent, she agreed to try. Two of the key lines were

> There are happy homes where music swells;
> There are flying sleighs, and jingling bells!

Because of the busy season, the Carriers Address was printed weeks in advance and left in stacks on a shelf at the newspaper office until the appointed delivery day. That didn't bother anyone. In Isabella's part of the country, there was *always* plenty of snow and jingling bells, so they were sure her poem would be a great success. Unfortunately, though Isabella prayed for snow, that particular year Christmas was smiled upon by a warm winter sun—with not one flake in sight!

The last day of the year was warm and clear—and utterly snowless. How could the paper release a "snow scene" poem on a snowless day? Isabella felt her reputation was at stake.

Her sister's husband was the editor of the paper, so she called a family meeting. "Oh, I'm sure," said the editor, "that the public will see the poetic license in this."

One of Isabella's sisters suggested a quick rewrite:

> There are happy homes where music swells,
> There are flying sleighs, that got stuck in the mud!

"It rhymes about like the rest and is more true to the season," she said.

"Why don't we burn the address and call the whole thing off for this year?" asked Isabella.

This started a family debate that ended with the conclusion that the carriers would be very disappointed not to have the tradition carried forward and not to receive the gifts from their customers.

Finally Isabella's father, sensing his daughter's distress, asked the editor if a footnote could be printed on those addresses. It could read, just below "flying sleighs and jingling bells": "If there ain't, there'd oughter be." The laughter that followed confirmed that everyone thought this was just the right answer to the problem.

And so, the next day, "flying sleighs" appeared with the footnote printed, and the address took the town by storm, so to speak. Isabella's reputation as a writer was saved.

May you find the same enjoyment and blessing in Isabella's writings as you read this story!

Robert L. Munce
June 1994

1

DELL'S RETURN HOME

*What I do thou knowest not now,
but thou shalt know hereafter.*

SHE was dressed in a plain, neat, buff linen traveling suit, and looked fresh and comfortable, despite the heat and dust of the August day. She stood in the doorway of a village railway depot, tapping the toe of one neatly booted foot on the sill of the door, in a manner that might have betokened impatience or restlessness. Turning occasionally, she let her bright eyes rove over the ill-built, ill-kept, never-cleaned room, where luckless travelers were doomed to pass their waiting time, and her rosy lip curled in a scornful or disgusted way; up the long, dusty hill leading to the depot buildings straggled a middle-aged man, with his hands in his pockets, and his straw hat on the back of his head. He quickened his pace a very little when he saw the fair picture framed in the doorway, and presently mounted the steps and stood before her, speaking in a tone that was half greeting and half surprise:

"Well, and so you are really here!"

The young lady, thus addressed, jumped down from the doorstep and, standing beside the man, reached up

1

and touched two rosy lips to his hard, brown cheek ere she answered:

"Didn't you expect me, Father?"

And now it is your turn to be surprised; you would never have guessed the relationship; this little lady was so dainty and neat and graceful, and the man was so rough and coarse and ungainly. He answered his daughter's question with a half laugh, half grumble:

"Oh, kind of, and kind of not; your fine folks out there have so bamboozled you up that I wasn't sure you would any of you remember that you had a father. Well, where's your luggage?"

"Here are my checks; there are two trunks, and there's a little box besides that's for you; Uncle Edward sent you some of grandma's choice books."

"Thank you for nothing," the man said gruffly. "We need a thousand things more than we do books. Old rubbish, not worth paying to have 'em carried home. I've a good mind to leave 'em here to be used for firewood."

The girl's bright eyes flashed, but she spoke in a cool, quiet tone:

"If you can't afford to have them carried down, Father, get a rope for me and bore a hole in the box, and I'll drag them home; I can as well as not."

Her father gave her a curious, puzzled look, but seemed to make nothing of her grave face.

"Oh, I'll have them taken down," he said at last. "But I don't set any great store by 'em myself. Your Uncle Edward heired all the reading taste there ever was in our family. Here, you, Bill Grimes," he added, raising his voice and beckoning to a man in the distance with a cart, "just give me a lift here, won't you? My team is away today."

The man drove around to the depot steps, and the

two were busy about trunks and bundles, the young man giving the dainty maiden sly glances whenever chance favored him, until she turned toward him and said, with frank kindness, "How do you do, Mr. Grimes; you remember me, don't you?" Then he doffed his cap, awkwardly enough, while the red blood mounted to his very hair, and could go no further, even when the elder man put his hands on his fat sides and shook with laughter.

"Mr. Grimes!" he ejaculated, when he could speak. "Now if that ain't the richest note!" and he went off into another laugh. "I reckon you ain't heard that name since before the old man died; have you, Bill? Come, come, Dell, you mustn't go to putting on airs here; you ain't down in Boston now, you must remember."

The imperturbable calm of the young girl's face and the composure of her voice seemed to awe her father into puzzled silence; she only said:

"I shall certainly try to call people by their right names, Father, here in Lewiston, just as I would anywhere else."

Her father's next remark was made when the last trunk was securely strapped to the cart. "Now we're ready; I guess you and I will jog on ahead, Dell." And the walk through the long, dusty, sleepy village streets was commenced.

The houses straggled at irregular and uncertain intervals, on either side of the street, and every single one of them looked as though the paint had been worn off by the third generation back; there were blinds hanging by one hinge, suggestive of many a delicious creak and groan when once the November wind had fair play among them. In the center of this delightful old town, there stood a great, square, weather-worn, sorrowful-looking wooden barn, named by courtesy a church; this seemed to be the climax to the forlorn picture, and to Dell Bronson's Boston-accustomed eyes, only her heart could tell how forlorn it all seemed. Her father, glancing furtively up at the still creature beside him, saw the wondering gaze that she cast about her and questioned, "How does it all look? natural like?"

"It looks," said Dell, speaking slowly and with great gravity, "as though all the people had gone away two hundred years ago, and never come back, and must have been glad of it ever since."

"Ha, ha, ho, ho!" chuckled the father. "You're a cute one, I guess; that's pretty good." And then they had reached their home.

Home! No, the wooden church had not been the climax after all. It was here in this long, low, once yellow-painted, now dirt-begrimed, wooden-shuttered, broken-windowed village tavern, with dirty piazzas running the entire length of the building, garnished with five wooden chairs, on which chairs lounged five of the most disgusting creatures that ever tilted back on the piazza of a third-rate hotel, and smoked, and chewed, and spit, and stared.

"Well, here you are, home at last," the father said as he pushed open the great yellow door.

Home! Was it actually her home? She shivered a little, not outwardly, and sped up the uncarpeted stairs without letting herself glance at any of the objects inside of that door.

The room into which she ushered herself was long and narrow; in one corner stood a single bedstead, on which was mounted a feather bed, suggestive of a sweltering night, and the finishing touch was a blue and green patchwork quilt, put on crooked. It was an indication of this girl's character that before she took off her hat and cloak, or even her gloves, she walked over to the bed and straightened the quilt, tucking it neatly in at the sides and then drawing it out again because, on the whole, it looked less forlorn drooping over the sides than it did to have it hidden away, thereby revealing the long, narrow, ungainly rails; then she shook up the mites of pillows and turned down the sheets in a dainty way. So much ere she took in the rest of the room; there was little enough to see: a queer, old-fashioned, twisted-legged table; a square wooden washstand with the paint worn off and with one leg shorter than the others, so that it tottled whenever it was touched, making a racket over the nicked washbowl and dingy pitcher; three chairs, one a dingy rocker, with a pitiful green and purple cushion on the seat; these completed the furnishing of the room, except, indeed, a faded red and green and yellow carpet, which in its best and brightest days could not have been pretty.

Dell untied the white cord that fastened the blue paper window curtain almost to the ceiling, and shut out the glaring sun, then went to the ten-inch looking glass and unfastened her hat, taking a grave, earnest look at her round, young face, with its rosy cheeks and great bright eyes. Not so bright but that one could detect a touch of sadness in their brown depths.

She sighed again, just a little touch of a sigh, quickly caught and suppressed, but there were visions of a little white and green room, in which she had stood only yesterday at this time; such a gem of a room, just those two colors, from the mossy carpet that pressed her feet, to the tiny sea-green bedstead in its dress of perfect white. Her own room it had been for several years. Uncle Edward's home, and Aunt Laura's, but nonetheless had it seemed hers. As she brushed her hair, she thought about it all.

Years and years ago, a lifetime ago it seemed to her, Uncle Edward had come and carried her away from this very room to her own green and white one in Boston. Seven years ago. Why, was it only seven? Yes, for she was almost eleven years old then, and now last month she was eighteen. She remembered the morning very well, and the weeks before that morning, and especially that one day in which her mother died; that white, tired mother, who never wore other than the sad, patient, gentle face in the midst of all her discouraging surroundings; and how discouraging they were! Dell was just beginning to have a faint gleam of an idea. Well, one day, suddenly, unexpectedly, after lying, for some weary weeks, on a high bed in a dreary room, having very little company in her loneliness and, Dell suspected now, anything but proper care, the burden of living was dropped, and for the first time in many years, the tired woman rested, body and heart and brain.

Dell remembered it all; remembered especially the solemn funeral, and how frightened and dreary the father looked, and how her tall, pale-faced Uncle Edward seemed to her to belong to another race of human beings. After the funeral, Aunt Nancy, her father's sister, came to live with him and assumed the endless cares of the dead woman, and Uncle Edward went back to his city home, taking Dell with him. She was his only sister's only child and had been to him in all respects as his own, never really given up to him by her father, yet the years had slipped by; and save once when she was nearly fourteen and had come to stay a week with her father, and had quarreled with Aunt Nancy in three days and been sent back to Boston, she had never left the beautiful home of her adoption, where she had been the carefully nurtured and much petted darling. By degrees it had nearly gone out of her life, the remembrance of any other home, until one day there had come a letter from her father, an unusual thing, for he was not given to letter writing. This one was brief, but startling. Thus it was in detail:

> *DEAR DELL:—This is to tell you that your Aunt Nancy is dead. She died three months ago, very sudden. Since which I have rubbed along alone, and it has been pretty rubbing work. What with the sass of the girls and breaking things, I'm about sick of it. If it so be that you are a mind to come home and do your duty by your father, why I'll be glad to see you, and will do my duty by you. But I shan't lay no commands on you. Them that has you, and has done for you, maybe thinks they has the best right to you, and if so be that you think so too, why so be it. If you decide to come, write and let me know, and I'll come to the cars and get you.*
>
> *Your obedient servant,*
> JONAS P. BRONSON.

This signature, not for any intended sarcasm, but from a vague memory that the few letters that he had been called upon to write closed in that manner.

Dell read this letter in the little summer parlor in Boston, standing leaning one arm on her piano, her white dress floating airily around her; read at first to herself, with a startled, shocked look on her face settling into one of such marked pain that the fair-faced woman, sitting in the low rocker by the window, said, "What is it, my darling?"

And Dell passed the letter to her without a word.

Now the next few sentences will tell you how this young girl had been nurtured, and upon what principles her actions were founded.

The lady read the letter and then said, in a quick, pained tone, "Oh, my darling child."

And Dell, still standing there, beside her beloved piano, said in a firm, clear voice, "Aunt Laura, when do you think I ought to go?"

A few minutes later, when Uncle Edward had joined them, he said, inquiringly, "There is no question as to your duty in this matter, Dell."

And she, raising her grave, earnest eyes to his face, answered, "Is there any room for doubt, Uncle Edward?"

"Will you tell me, my dear child, what thought you have in your heart, that decides the matter for you so promptly?"

And the young girl, with eyes drooping and fast filling with great tears, still answered, steadily:

"Honor thy father and thy mother."

So here she was in that long, narrow room, brushing her hair before the ten-inch glass. Is it a wonder she sighed a little over the contrast? But Dell Bronson was not a girl that was much given to sighing. She gave some energetic twists to her wavy hair and then addressed herself aloud, which she was rather in the habit of doing:

"It isn't a palace by any means, but then it is my father's house, and I shall live in it, and be happy besides, if there is any such thing."

With the expression "my father's house," a bright smile broke over her face, and she repeated aloud and slowly, "'In my Father's house there are many mansions. I go to prepare a place for you.' Oh, Dell Bronson, you must not forget that your Father's house is a palace, and that you are a King's daughter; never mind the place in which you may have to stay for a little while, just to make your preparations, you know. There are a great many things to do."

Meantime Bill Grimes had appeared with her trunks, and they had been brought up to her room; so diving into the depths of one of them, she produced therefrom a white, daintily ruffled apron, and tying it on she ran gaily downstairs, more gaily than she felt, to conceal an aching desire at her heart for a loving greeting from somebody. Oh, for another to clasp tender arms about her! She felt young to begin life alone. Yet at that moment there came a bright memory to her heart, of One who loved her with a love "passing that of women." She remembered his eternal promise, "As one whom his mother comforteth, so will I comfort you." And the gaiety had toned down into a steady, sweet brightness by the time she opened the dining-room door.

2

THE YOUNG MISTRESS

Whatsoever thy hand findeth to do.

IT was anything but an inviting picture upon which her eyes rested—that long, dreary dining room—with the sun pouring in as blindingly as it could, through cobwebby, fly-stained windows, slanting its beams toward the table, spread for supper. Dell went resolutely toward that table and made her eyes take in all the details. It is safe to say that she received there her first knowledge as to how wretched a thing a table set for supper could be made to look. The cloth was stained with coffee and tea and daubed with egg and molasses and gravy; the sun had accomplished a melting process with the butter, and five or six flies had found oily graves; the bread was evidently that which had been cut at noon and left over and, being unable to melt, had taken to drying instead; the flies were holding a perfect carnival over the uncovered sugar bowls, apparently never missing those who were sailing around in the milk pitchers. In a certain house in Boston, there was one of the daintiest of dining rooms, with a bay window all aglow with geraniums, and tea roses, and one great white lily; it was next to impossible that Dell should not think of that dining room and of the vacant side where she sat, only last evening. She thought of it, but the thought did not appear in her words. She gathered up the skirt of her buff linen dress about her, looked at the floor, and said, "Oh, my patience! I wonder if I have enough of that commodity for this occasion? It is too late to mop, but there are several other things to be done—first, though, where is Father?" Nobody was in the dining room, and, after hesitating a moment, she stepped across the hall to the barroom; there were five or six loungers who looked at her as if she had been an apparition. Confused by her unusual position, it was some minutes before she could single her father out from among the group, whose feet were disposed around the room on the backs of chairs and settees. When she did, she promptly summoned him to a conference in the hall.

"Father," she said, closing the door on the staring men, with a little gesture of disgust, "am I the housekeeper?"

Then her father stared and finally chuckled. "I dunno about that," he said at last. "I shouldn't wonder if Sally thinks she is."

"Who is Sally?"

"She's the cook, and you'll have to do about right if you don't want to get turned out, and like enough you'll get turned out anyhow, if her back happens to get up about anything. I've been expecting leave to go, off and on, these three months."

"But, Father, I want to be housekeeper myself. I can't do anything for your comfort unless I am mistress, and I want to have things different. It isn't comfortable in there!" This with an inclination of her head toward the dining room.

Her father shrugged his shoulders expressively. "No

more it ain't," he said earnestly. "I've 'most forgot the meaning of the word. Why, Dell, I ain't had no comfort since your mother died."

There was a plaintive sound to his voice as he repeated the last sentence impressively that brought tears to Dell's eyes.

"Poor Father," she said, with a gentle caressing touch of her hand on his coat sleeve. "Well, we'll have things different after awhile. Then I am to be mistress, am I?"

Whereupon her father shook his head again. "I dunno about that; you must keep on the right side of Sally, and Kate she ain't far behind—though I do think she ain't quite so obstreperous like."

"Who is Kate?"

"Well, she's the chambermaid, and dining room girl, and maid-of-all-work; sort of pretty decent kind of a girl when she ain't mad, which she is mostly."

"But, Father, I want it the other way. I want them to be trying to keep on the right side of me!"

Mr. Bronson looked thoughtfully down at the young creature before him, then presently he laughed.

"What would you do if they should both flare up and leave?" he asked with the air of one who had presented a formidable trouble, but her answer was prompt and decided.

"Get others in their place, of course."

"And s'pose they sass you and don't pay no attention to your notions?"

"Then I should dismiss them."

There really seemed to be something refreshing to the father in his daughter's brisk, bright words and ways; he looked down at her admiringly and chuckled his answer:

"You're pretty cute, I guess. Well, fight it out with

Sally and Kate, if you can; I'll back you. But you'll get sick of it, and dodge, and leave things go to everlasting smash, as I have." But even as he said this, he had a dim notion that this daughter of his was different from himself and would be very likely to accomplish what she undertook; and as he went back to that horrid barroom, he winked confidently to old Joe Simmons and said, "She's a brick, now I tell you."

As for Dell, she went directly to the kitchen. Oh, the kitchen! Adjectives would fail in their attempt to describe it. Dell, on the threshold, paused and said in an undertone of dismay, "Shall I ever be able to eat any more dinners as long as I live?" Then seeing that the two slatternly beings who occupied the space between the stove and the sink had each two sharp eyes, she stepped forward and spoke pleasantly:

"How do you do? I know your names, but I don't know just which of you owns each name. Which is Sally and which is Kate, please?"

The red-haired creature answered, with arms pressed against her fat sides, "I'm Sally, and her's Kate. Do you want anything out here?"

"Several things," was Dell's prompt answer. "In the first place, Sally, I want to know if you have any clean tablecloths?"

"Perhaps I has, and perhaps I hasn't. What about it?"

"Only that Kate and I want a clean one right away; we're going to set the table over again, and that cloth in there is all ready for your washtub."

Kate giggled, and Sally frowned.

"The table is set for supper," she said wrathfully. "And it is about time to have it, and it's going to be had too, and folks as doesn't belong to the kitchen had better keep out and not spoil their fine clothes."

Dell's voice was clear and firm, and yet gentle.

"Then we'll delay supper for half an hour and get the table into proper order; and, Sally, I may as well explain to you now that I am Mr. Bronson's daughter, and I have come here to take charge of his house. I am very much obliged for you doing it all the while; it must have been hard for you to have had so much care, and a great deal of work besides, but now I have come home to share the work, and I hope it will not be very hard for either of us."

Sally's face had grown ominously dark during this little speech, gracefully worded and gently spoken though it was, and at its close she burst forth:

"Indeed, and I think it won't be hard for me any longer. I'll not do another stroke of work in this house. I'll not be bossed about by any red-cheeked chit like you. I'll tell you that."

Ere she had done speaking, Dell's hand was in her pocket. She drew forth her *porte monnaie* and spoke in a calm, dignified tone:

"Very well. How much do I owe you?"

Poor, cross Sally! Her favorite weapon, which she had held over the heads of so many helpless mistresses, with which she had, endless times, driven poor Mr. Bronson back to the barroom in despair, had never before met with such a response. She stood silent and dismayed, whereat Kate could not forbear giggling again.

Dell saw her advantage and with rare diplomacy followed it up. With quiet dignity she returned her *porte monnaie* to her pocket and spoke gently and pleasantly:

"I will overlook your improper language to me, Sally, because I see you have allowed yourself to become angry. I will even give you time to change your mind; if, after thinking the matter over, you decide that you want to try whether we cannot get along comfortably together and be helps to each other, we will say no more about this; but if you still want to go, you may come to me tomorrow morning for your wages."

Then she turned instantly to Kate, with a bright smile. "Now, Kate, if you will get that tablecloth, you and I will set to work and see how soon we can get supper ready."

Then she left the kitchen, in some doubt as to whether she would see either Kate or the tablecloth, but she set resolutely to work clearing the dishes to a side table, and presently Kate appeared with a beautifully clean tablecloth hanging over her arm. Dell's eyes fastened upon it in genuine pleasure. It was possible then to have something clean.

"Who does the ironing?" she asked, eagerly, as they spread out the cloth with its crisp, fresh folds.

"I does, mostly," Kate answered. "I irons the tablecloths."

"It is beautifully done," the young mistress said brightly. "I never saw one look nicer than this."

Kate's face broke into a broad, pleased smile; it was new to her to hear words of commendation; she tramped briskly about, doing Dell's bidding with an air of satisfaction, and Dell, as she looked at her round, homely face, knew that Kate's heart was won.

They were very busy during the next half hour; with some pleasant explanation, one improvement after another was suggested. The knives rubbed a little, a damp cloth taken to the glass sugar bowl, fresh milk pitchers brought, freshly cut cakes of butter on glittering squares of ice, freshly cut plates of bread, the goblets washed until they shone.

"It do make a difference," Kate said philosophically,

and Dell thought it did; she could hardly make it seem the same table that she had surveyed half an hour before. A few more touches and the supper was ready.

"Do you wait on the table?" Dell asked of Kate, with many an inward misgiving as to the girl's slatternly appearance. Maggie, the girl who waited at Aunt Laura's table, was such a picture of neatness. But if she had but known it, Kate looked much better than usual, having smoothed her hair and put on a net in honor of the expected newcomer. She remembered it, and conscious of her superior appearance, she answered, blandly:

"I does."

"Then I believe we're ready; aren't we, Sally? I'll take in your tea cakes, Kate, while you roll down your sleeves, and—do you wear white aprons? You have one, haven't you? Suppose you run and get it then, and I'll ring the bell."

"La!" said Kate, with a touch of grumness. "Yes, I has one, but I don't wear it; they does not care; if I only gives them tea enough and bread and butter, that's all they wants; they doesn't know whether my apron be white or black."

"Very likely," Dell said, with unfailing good humor. "But then, you see, we care, and we want to have everything very nice tonight. Do you iron aprons as nicely as you do tablecloths? Run and get yours on, until I see if you do." And Kate, much to her own astonishment, went.

The tea bell rang, and they lounged in from the barroom and piazza; among them two brisk young clerks, who had just come, one from the post office, and the other from the store. Dell, in the pantry, just off the dining room, waited to watch Kate's movements and heard the comments. The two clerks sat opposite each other, and they looked into each other's astonished eyes.

"I say, Tom," one of them ejaculated, "the millennium's come. Did you know it? Clean cloth, clean knives, and no flies in the milk, as true as you're alive."

"Yes, and look at the butter, will you? 'Tisn't the millennium, it's paradise." This was his companion's response.

Dell heard their comments and smiled and sighed. Smiled over their evident satisfaction, and sighed to think that perhaps this was really their highest idea of that paradise which their tongues so lightly syllabled.

Presently her father came in, and Dell watched eagerly to see if he would note the changes. He took his accustomed seat, looked slowly down the length of the table, and then deliberately arose and, lounging out to the kitchen sink, washed his hands; then, disappearing for a moment, returned with his hair brushed and a linen coat covering his soiled shirtsleeves, and Dell gleefully clapped her hands over this emphatic comment on the new order of things.

Alone in her room that night, she tried to think calmly about this new life that had opened to her. She tried to shut out that fair, green room, with its dainty belongings, the luxurious home, in its elegant beauty, appealing to every one of her delicately educated senses—tried to shut out the vivid sense of the difference between the pure, pale, refined, life-ennobled face of her Uncle Edward and the uncultured, stolid face of her father; failing in both these efforts she turned resolutely away from them all, and drawing from her pocket her tiny Bible, she read about that other home of hers, where they had no need of the sun in his glory, because of the eternal glory that was beyond all earthly brightness; and about the other Father of hers, the shining of whose face was the light of heaven, read until her own face shone with the reflection of all this unutterable grandeur, and earthly homes and friends faded and were forgotten.

3

THE LETTER AND THE VISITOR

I will guide thee with mine eye.

BEFORE Dell had been at home a week, she received one morning a letter from her Uncle Edward. She rushed with it to her own room and fairly hugged it to her heart, and covered the soiled envelope and inky postage stamp with kisses before she set about devouring its contents. How delightfully familiar the smooth, flowing letters looked:

BOSTON, *August 15, 18—.*
MY DEAR DELL,—Dear daughter, I had nearly said, so much does it seem to me that I am writing to my own child; but even while I sighed to remember that you are not my daughter, and therefore not with us today, I rejoiced over the thought that you are a daughter of the eternal God, and that your Father has you in his constant care and keeping.

Your Aunt Laura sends love and a wish for your presence because of canned fruit or fruit that is to be canned, or something of that sort;

not, of course, for any other reason. We attended the concert last evening without you; that part was sad; the concert was fine. Do you think much, during these concert days, which you were to enjoy, of the great multitude, which no man can number, clothed in white, and with palms in their hands, who sing with a loud voice, and cease not day or night? I thought of it last evening. Your Aunt Laura leaned forward to me during one of the parts in which we had expected to hear your voice, and said, "She will not be missing from the other concert. When the ten thousand times ten thousand and thousands of thousands sing the triumphal song, our Dell will join the chorus"; and I answered her: "There is more to it even than that. I trust, because of her not being with us tonight, that there will be added voices to that chorus." Have you thought of it, Dell? Perhaps the Father called you to that part of his vineyard just now in order that you might induce some singers to join in the song that the redeemed from every nation and kindred and people and tongue shall sing. Dear Dell, don't go alone. I am sure there are people in Lewiston, who have not thought about it, who yet will be glad to go with you when you press them to join you; and the thought brings me to the main reason why I am writing this letter in some haste, this morning, instead of being in my counting room. God has opened a wonderful door to you. Do you remember the sentence in your Father's letter, "No drunkard shall inherit the kingdom of heaven"? You have been carefully and prayerfully taught that truth until I think you feel it in all its fullness, and now

the Father has called you to one of the centers
where this truth is unknown or disregarded, that
you may work and think and pray for the turning of tempted feet into the narrow path. I glory
in your call, dear child; be worthy of your
commission. When he calls you home to give
him your statement of the work, be sure that you
have no undone duty pressing your conscience,
and see to it in that hour you are not found
standing idle. I did not mean to preach a sermon,
dear child; that is not my vocation, you know. I
only mean to give you little hints, here and there,
of the peculiar trust the Lord must have in you
to have given you thus early in life so wide and
solemn a working place in his garden.

I think you have learned so well whose
daughter you are, and what the King expects of
his child, and how blessed that child is in having
the great King for a Father, that perhaps, it is
quite unnecessary to remind you of the great
and eager longing that there should be in your
heart for your earthly father. Carry the desire
about with you constantly, the longing to see
him one day moving triumphantly among that
countless throng. No, my dear Dell, that is bad
advice—I mean, tell the great longing of your
heart out freely to your Elder Brother, and ask
his daily, hourly help. Do you know that I have
put myself in such a position that I cannot help
you in this matter? I mean, of course, by personal
help. Your father will hear no word from me,
because that word affects his business. At present
it seems wiser for me to cease from personal
effort; when you have reached that point the
King will make it known to you. Do not be

afraid of entering doors that he has himself opened.

There is much to say, and, as usual, very little time in which to say it. Is there less time in Boston than elsewhere, I wonder? Your class in Sabbath school troubles me; they do not seem to assimilate with Miss Terry. The truth is she wears too much bracelet, makes too marked a difference between her own toilet and that of her girls. Do you think it would do to give her a quiet little hint of the trouble? If she were only Dell Bronson now, I could say it to her in all frankness, and I think she would receive it. I do not mean Dell Bronson receiving a bit of truth from her Uncle Edward, but Dell Bronson receiving it from her superintendent, or from anyone who meant it for her good, or, broader than that, from those who do not mean it for her good, so she could gather good from it. You told me once that I thought too highly of you; don't allow me to; dear Dell, grow far beyond my thinking, or even hoping. There are glorious possibilities of grace to be attained—a possible flight high enough for the ambition of an angel. Advise me, please, in regard to Miss Terry.

Joe Turner still continues to pinch his next neighbor black and blue every Sabbath afternoon, so the neighbor says, and resolutely refuses to show any indications of civilization. Your Aunt Laura and I have taken him for our special subject of prayer. At home all is as usual, except the one great void made by your absence. Baby Laura has a new pearl, small and white, which she constantly uses, on rattle, or silver dollar, or her luckless holder's finger, as the case may be. I meant this letter to be brief, and it will not terminate; there is no way but to cut it short. One word about the main thought in it: If you are at a loss how to proceed, which way to turn, remember your Father's letter of full and explicit instructions. Go to it and him for direction; following this rule, there is no possibility of mistakes. Good morning, dear child.

Your loving *UNCLE*.

Dell folded the letter with a look on her face made up of eagerness and dismay. There was a little rush of tears to her eyes, but she brushed them quickly away and indulged in her favorite employment, talking to herself.

"What a singular letter that would be if it came from anyone in this world but Uncle Edward! The idea of congratulating me upon the door opened for me! Now, my opinion would be that the door of temperance was shut, and bolted, and barred. Who ever heard of the daughter of a rum seller living in a hotel preaching temperance?" Dell's cheeks glowed as she spoke, and her lips quivered, yet this was the bare, undeniable fact, and such was her nature that she had to face disagreeable truths, plainly and firmly, in order to endure them at all.

"What on earth can I do?" she continued with eager tongue. "If I were only a girl in a book, now, there would be no end to the wonders that I could perform. I should go on bended knees to my father and with tears in my eyes implore him not to sell any more rum, and immediately he would shed tears and promise to listen to my petition; then we two would empty all the rum barrels and convert the village, and then travel around and convert the world. That is the way book girls do; but, most unfortunately, I am not that style of girl; and even if I were, it would do no sort of good to beg my father to give up a money-making business. Did not my poor mother's pale face beg for that every day of her life? I wish Uncle Edward had been more explicit; he must be right—he generally is; but what in the world I can do for the cause of temperance, situated as I am at present, is more than I can imagine. A more utterly hopeless cause could not be given me. My very eagerness to do something makes my powerlessness all the more plain."

She was pacing up and down her room now with the eager look changed to one of perplexed thought. The letter had aroused the one great burden always crouched at her heart. Her father was a rum seller, a respectable, licensed drunkard maker. She, Dell Bronson, who had been brought up in her uncle's house to utterly loathe and abhor the sight of liquor, to refuse its use in any shape or form, to work and plan and pray for its banishment from the civilized world, must every day face an army of rum drinkers, must hear their silly jokes as she passed through the halls, must lie awake at night and listen to their drunken songs, or quarrels, or oaths, must pass by homes made wretched by the daily presence of the demon, and remember that her father furnished the poison at so much a glass; must watch his own face grow redder, his eyes more bleared, his steps more uncertain every day, and yet be absolutely powerless and helpless. She fairly groaned as the vivid picture of all this came before her. Did she remember that fearful sentence, "No drunkard shall inherit the kingdom of heaven"? Oh! did she not? Sometimes it seemed written in letters of fire all over the walls of this licensed hotel. How Dell hated that word "licensed" nobody knew. "No drunkard," and her father not only made drunkards, but the law pronounced it a legitimate business. Actually trafficked in souls at so much a soul! No, not even that, but reckoned them in masses, these souls that must live on and on for ever; gave a man the right to ruin just as many of them as he possibly could, provided he paid for the privilege a few dollars a year. "What can I do?" she said, in anguish of soul, as her heart sickened at the thought of all this, and at the added anguish that her father had bought the privilege of barring his own soul out of heaven, as well as that of others.

"What does Uncle Edward think it possible for me to do? Why didn't he tell me? If he only realized, as I do, that I can do nothing, *nothing.*" Then her eye fell on the closing lines in the letter: "If you are at a loss how to proceed, which way to turn, remember your Father's letter of full and explicit instructions. Go to it and him for direction; following this rule there is no possibility of mistakes."

And as she reread the words, gradually the look of pain died out from her face, and there came first a calm and then a smile.

"My Father's letter," she said softly. "I am constantly forgetting that my Father is watching and planning, and is more interested than I can be. Uncle Edward is right. He must have something that he intends me to do, else he would not have called me here; I wonder what my instructions are and where I shall look for them." She unclasped her little Bible, not with any definite end in view, for she knew she had no time, just then, to search for directions, but from a kind of habit that she had of picking up the little book and just glancing at some earnest word or loving promise; but her whole face flushed and her eyes brightened as they caught the sentence, "I will instruct thee, and

teach thee, in the way which thou shalt go: I will guide
thee with mine eye." The promise was not new to her;
it only came suddenly home to her heart for that
wondrous power that every lover of the Bible understands, a power that makes it seem as though those
particular words were spoken just then by some wonderfully distinct voice, and spoken for you entirely and
only. Dell instantly shut her Bible and dropped upon
her knees, and the first sentences of her prayer were:
"My Father, it is enough; I yield myself to thee;
instruct and guide me as thou wilt; lead where thou
wilt; thy daughter is ready to follow thee whitherso-
ever thou goest. Ah, dear Father, perhaps I am not, I
don't know, but make me willing; make me all that
thou wouldst have me."

Five minutes afterward she was summoned to the
tearoom to see a caller. This same tearoom deserves a
word on its own account; it was an emanation of Dell's
brain, not the room exactly, but its belongings and
uses. It was a little square room with a side door
leading into the yard, and had been bare of furniture,
and had been appropriated at no better use than to
serve as a sort of general storeroom for umbrellas,
overcoats, hats, rubbers, shawls, anything that might be
needed on a rainy day. Dell had seized upon it, banished the rubbish to appropriate dark closets, dragged
to light enough carpeting to cover its bit of floor,
hung the windows in cream color, repapered the walls,
brought from the attic an old table with three legs,
coaxed the hostler into adding a fourth, covered it
daintily with an old cream-colored curtain, brought
from her mother's room an old worn chair, stuffed and
padded its back, seat, and sides, and dressed it in cloth
of the same creamy tint; filled the window-seat with
little pots of sweet-smelling flowers brought from her

Boston home, strewed the table with bright, inviting books, and altogether converted the former store-room into one of the daintiest, softest, sunniest, and quietest of little rooms that her father at least had ever seen. Dell, in writing to Aunt Laura about it, said: "I call it the 'Tearoom,' for reasons that I will explain to you when my plans are fully developed. But, between you and me, it might be more appropriately called the 'Trap Room,' and I mean it to wage war against that fearful barroom. How, shall, with many other things, be told you hereafter."

It had cost her two days of hard labor, and her last act had been to lay the two daily papers that Uncle Edward had sent her on the little cream-colored table and inform her father, when she called him to survey the room, that he would always find the latest papers on that table, and the armchair vacant at any hour of the day. So when she entered the room on this particular morning and beheld her father cozily seated in the armchair, engaged in tearing the wrapper from the late paper, she flushed with pleasure and felt that her trap had commenced its work. Her caller was a wee sprite of a child, daintily done up in a pique dress, with blue ribbons floating at her waist and among her brown curls. Small, and sweet, and shy, with a winning ladylike shyness, her voice was as clear as a flute's when she looked with her truthful blue eyes into Dell's brown ones and said:

"If you please, Miss Bronson, will you sign my temperance pledge?"

4

SIGNING THE PLEDGE

Thou art my Father, my God.

DELL looked with amused eyes on the dainty little roll of pique and ribbon, and then suddenly glanced toward her father. Evidently he had heard the little lady's petition, for he shook out his paper with a disgusted air and muttered something that his daughter could not catch.

For one moment she stood irresolute; it was a queer place to come to for signers to a temperance pledge, but the innocent little morsel, looking up at her, did not appreciate the difficulties. Dell's mind was very promptly made up. The first thing to do had come to her, and she meant to do it.

"Certainly I will sign it," she said in a bright voice. "Why, you have several names here already; well, I will put mine down and then you will have seven," and she moved with a brisk step toward the little writing table.

Her father spoke suddenly and more sternly than he had ever before spoken to her:

"Dell! What tomfoolery are you about now?"

Dell waited until her rapid fingers had glided over the blank space and left the name Dell Bronson in unmistakably clear letters before she answered cheerily:

"I'm signing a temperance pledge, Father."

"Temperance, fiddlesticks!" Mr. Bronson said angrily, while Dell serenely folded the pledge and returned it to the little maiden.

"Are you going to put your name on that thing?"

"I have done so, Father."

"Well, it is a pretty business for you to be about, I should think. You ain't in Boston now, and I reckon you better remember it. If your Uncle Edward hasn't taught you anything but to go against your father in this fashion, you may as well go back to him. I won't have such doings going on here, and you may as well know it first as last!"

The little buff pique cast a frightened glance at the surly looking man, hurriedly thrust the pledge into her mite of a basket, and moved briskly toward the door.

Dell bowed and smiled her out, promised, in an undertone, to be present at the evening meeting if she could, then came back to her father.

He had taken up his paper, but he still grumbled, and waxing louder as he received no answer, at last his words became distinct again.

"Do you know what you are about?"

"I'm dusting and rearranging this table. What is the matter, Father?"

"Matter! Don't you know enough to know that these meddling fools, who are sneaking around with pledges and coaxing folks to come to their confounded meetings, are trying to ruin my business?"

"No, sir, that isn't their object; they're trying to save drunkards."

"Save fools!" said the man, very crossly, and Dell answered promptly:

"Yes, sir; they are undoubtedly fools, or they wouldn't need saving; but that's what we are trying to do."

"Well, I don't choose to have a girl of mine make a fool of herself."

"No, sir, I haven't the slightest intention of doing so. I have signed the pledge, you know."

The newspaper was angrily flung on the floor at this point, and the rough father said in his roughest tone:

"You talk like a fool! You had no business to put your name to that paper."

Dell turned from her dusting and looked with two bright, steady eyes at her father and spoke very quietly:

"Why not?"

"Why not! Don't you know I get my living, and yours, by selling rum?"

Truly Dell knew that—knew it to her bitter sorrow and shame. Her cheeks flushed, but she answered, still steadily:

"Yes, sir."

"And you want to help break down my business, do you? Pretty way to treat the business that clothes and feeds you!"

"Father," said Dell, with a clear voice and very determined eyes, "do you want me to sell rum?"

"No, of course not," he said testily. "Nobody asked you to sell anything. What I want is—"

But she quietly interrupted him.

"Do you want me to *drink* it?"

And then there came to this father a sudden shiver as he fancied this bright, handsome daughter of his standing in his barroom drinking his liquor. He answered her in a very snarly way, but still promptly and decidedly:

"No, I *don't.*"

"Very well, sir; I've promised not to do either; that is what I meant by signing the pledge. It is not, by any means, the first one I have signed. I am very sorry that rum selling is your business. I would be willing to live on bread and water, and work hard for that, if you would give it up. I am not in sympathy with it in the least. I expect to do everything in my power to hinder the sale and the use of rum. I don't mean to use it in any possible form. I mean to talk against it, and work against it, and pray against it, as long as I live."

It was a long speech for Dell to make. In some respects it was a strange one for a daughter to address to her father, but Dell, you remember, had been most carefully educated on the very subject; she could not help having a pretty thorough knowledge of her father's character; she could not help feeling the marked difference between him and her Uncle Edward. She had resolved on a very straightforward course in speaking of this subject with her father. She knew that she would have to go contrary to his views in many ways, in nothing perhaps more frequently than in this matter. It surely was best to show her colors most decidedly at this first opportunity and await the consequence. Her father was much less angry than she had supposed he would be. He knew much better than she did the very low ebb at which the temperance cause stood in the village. He knew *he* had supporters many and strong; he did not in the least fear the influence of the temperance people; they irritated him, but he contented himself with calling them "fools" and "fanatics" and a few other rough and harmless names; and sneering at their efforts, which, be it known, were faint and weak enough to almost call for sneers instead of commendation, even from friends of the cause.

Dell's outburst half-angered, half-amused him. She looked so pretty standing there before him in her dainty dress, her bright eyes flashing and her cheeks a brilliant red, so pretty and so utterly harmless, he could certainly afford to laugh, albeit he did it in a sneering way.

"Mighty becoming your hysterics are to you. I s'pose that's the reason your uncle trained you in 'em; he always had an eye for them kind of things. Well, well, you must have something to do, I s'pose, and I've no kind of objection to your amusing yourself in this fashion if you want to, so long as you don't plague me about it; an awful sight of good you'll find your talking and thinking and whatnot will do, and folks will call you a fool for trying to knock out your own under-pinning; but that's neither here nor there if you're suited." And having talked himself into comparative good humor, Mr. Bronson lounged out of the room.

Dell stood where he had left her, looking after him; she drew two or three quick, hard breaths. This, then, was her father! It rushed upon her with new and overwhelming force, the gulf between them; there was no common ground on which they met; in not one single thing could they seem to sympathize. Oh, to be at home once more, in her own beautiful room, to feel herself again the center and joy of her uncle's home, to escape from these surroundings, the great hot kitchen, with its cross and filthy serving girls, the dining room, with all the rough, ungainly set who gathered there to eat and stare, that awful barroom with the smoking, spitting, drinking crew! Couldn't she go? How they missed her there, in that beautiful home. Who would miss her here? Her father would not object to her going back; indeed she had a vague feeling that he disliked the sort of restraint that he almost instinctively put upon himself in her presence. She knew that in some respects he was half afraid of her. She knew that she would only have to go to him with a determined air and announce her intention of returning to Boston by the afternoon train. He would stare, and frown a little, and grumble, and very likely he would even swear, but it would end in sending Jo to the cars with her trunks. She knew it was too thoroughly understood that she was her Uncle Edward's adopted child, to have her movements absolutely forbidden, or even very closely questioned.

Should she go? The thought, the possibility, made her heart beat hard and fast, and for a moment it seemed to her that she must go at once—that very hour. But then. Ah, me! How all the difficulties and reasons why rushed in the moment she lifted the gate and let in that innocent-sounding "but then." She looked around that cheery little morning room which her skill and determination had brought to pass. How pure and sweet it was in the very center of this dreary old tavern. Must there not be something refining in the atmosphere and surroundings of the room—this little bit of her Boston home, set down here? *Wouldn't* he feel the difference after awhile? She thought of that dining room, clean and neat, almost bright now. What a dreadful room it was that first time she looked in on it! The thought of the changes wrought in the kitchen—of the wine she had banished from the pudding sauces—of the brandy bottle, filled for culinary purposes, that she had deliberately smashed; not much was this to do. Certainly, very little could be gained so long as the hated poisons were so freely poured at the table, but there were at least two of the men who did not drink liquor at the table; they at least would not have the taste for it fostered by the food that they ate. There were numerous other changes that she had made and that she contemplated making. And, besides all this, was he not after all her very own father? Should she desert him? She who that very morning prayed so earnestly to be helped and guided? Should she weakly yield the struggle and run back to rest and peace?

No, she wouldn't. He was her father, ignorant and coarse and degraded though he was; despite the chewing, and the spitting, and the smoking, and the drinking, though his clothing and body were so permeated with the fumes of tobacco, though his breath was so choked with the fumes of liquor that it made her faint to go near him—still she was his only child. There was no possibility of getting away from that fact. It made her fairly tremble with pain to think of it. What fathers she knew! grand, noble men. How lovingly she had seen some daughters lean on their father's arm; how reverently she had heard them pronounce the dear name! Her heart fairly ached with the pain, and the longing, and the hopelessness. And then suddenly over this gloom there broke Dell's rich, sweet smile; a sudden thought had pressed home to her heart, a sudden mingling of sweet and true and wonderful words, mingling with and breaking up the sadness:

"My Father, thou art the guide of my youth."

Did an angel whisper those words in her ear? They sounded lovingly through her brain; she had longed for a father to lean upon, such as she had known other girls to have. She had sighed bitterly over her low estate. She had forgotten for a moment whose child she was. The King's daughter! She must not forget that. Truly she had a Father whom not only all the earth but all heaven adored. Oh, yes! she could ask counsel of *her* Father. She could be guided by him in all things. He could not be mistaken; he would never die and leave her; he would never, never take his supporting arm away from her. Surely she could smile and be glad.

She's a sharp one, Mr. Bronson told himself as he walked toward the barroom. *Let her have her notions; who cares? Don't hurt nobody. Won't do to treat her as if she was a baby, or a common kind of a girl—for she ain't, that's so. She'll be scooting off to Boston first thing I know if I don't mind my p's and q's, and I should miss her, now that's a fact; things ain't never gone so smoothlike in this house, not since her mother died. As for them silly notions about temperance, she can't do no harm, and she'll get over 'em. They think it makes 'em big and independent. Besides, I don't want her to drink; it's a nasty habit for women. I never kept no woman-kind about me that would drink. I won't have 'em. I don't think it's decent.* And Mr. Bronson drew himself up virtuously and went straight to the bar and prepared himself a glass of brandy.

As for Dell, she went to the kitchen and made her father the daintiest little pudding that milk and eggs and sugar and fruit, beaten and mashed and foamed, and otherwise mysteriously compounded, could produce.

5

THE TEMPERANCE MEETING

Who hath despised the day of small things.

ALL the while Dell was dressing for the temperance meeting, there was in her heart a sense of pleasure at the thought of meeting friends and coworkers. She had been used to many friends and much work—hearty, earnest, enthusiastic work. She was used to accompanying her Uncle Edward to the great hall in Boston and mingling there with a throng of interested workers. She liked the whole of it—the music, the brilliant lights, the enthusiastic people, the eloquent speakers. She had missed it all. She was glad to enter into it again with all her heart.

She thought about it as she went briskly down the straggling street of the village toward the church. Thought about it until her hand was on the doorknob and she pushed open the door. Then what a sudden coming down from the clouds it was! Instead of the great hall brilliant with light, and glowing with flowers, and alive with well-dressed throngs of expectant people who poured in unceasingly amid the subdued tremble of wonderful music, there was that dingy, dusty, dismal church, smelling as if the united breaths of worshipers of a hundred years back were entombed there, and lighted by those sputtering, hissing, smoking kerosene lamps; and the audience was composed of five boys, two of whom were playing football with their caps, a young man who was preparing with the aid of his jackknife and a bit of chip to trim the aforesaid lamps, two girls who whispered and giggled in one of the dark corners, and the dainty little bundle of pique, Dell's morning acquaintance.

Now, that young lady was of course aware that the village in which she was at present living was very different in many respects from Boston. She knew it boasted of no public hall, and certainly the tumbledown old church building was far enough from deceiving her as to its condition; but, then, she had lived all of her grown-up life in Boston, and public meetings of any sort had to do, in her mind, with gas-illuminated buildings, and swelling organs, and throngs of people. She found she had been considering them as necessities. She stood still by the door, trying to take in the situation. What a great bewildering disappointment it was! Where was the meeting? Where were the people to make it of? At last, she did what Dell was very apt to do on trying occasions—she laughed, not very loud, but merrily; the extreme ludicrousness of the whole thing and the absurdity of her own expectations had just crept over her. Her laugh ended, she cast about her as to ways and means. She brought the game of hat ball to a sudden termination by an abrupt question, addressed to the larger of the two boys:

"Is your name Johnny?"

"No, ma'am," he said, wondering but respectful. "It's Tommy though."

"Oh, it is! Well, Tommy Though, what do you suppose is the reason that you and I don't let down some of these windows? How long do you suppose it will be before we will bake if we stay in this oven?"

"I don't know," he answered, laughing; "but my name is Tommy Truman."

"Is it indeed! What a splendid name. Are you Tommy True boy, as well as man?"

"I don't know," he said again, this time with a little touch of admiring thoughtfulness in his voice.

"You must be that if you mean to be the other. Really and truly you know, as well as in name. But about the windows. Aren't we equal to them? Is your name Tommy, too?" This to the younger boy, who turned toward her with a roguish but not ungraceful bow and answered:

"I'm Harry Mason, at your service, ma'am."

"Thank you; then you want to know how you can serve me, of course. If you will go to the other side of the church and open every window, I shall consider myself delightfully served."

He started at once, but suddenly turned back with a puzzled air. "How shall I keep them up? There's no fastening nor anything."

"Ah! That's the question! I don't know; it shall be part of your service to find out."

The boy laughed, but went at once to work, and Tommy Truman was dispatched to the row of windows on the opposite side. Meantime the lamps, after infinite pains and some burning of fingers, were trimmed and sputtered less, but looked dim and threatening. The young man turned toward Dell.

"Good evening. I shall have to introduce myself. My name is Nelson; I am bookkeeper at the factory. And this is Miss—?"

"Bronson, from the hotel," Dell explained as he hesitated inquiringly.

"I beg pardon," he said with a little flush on his face; "you are not connected with Mr. Bronson who keeps the hotel?"

"I am his daughter," Dell answered quietly. Then, her eyes gleaming with mischief, "Where's the temperance meeting, Mr. Nelson?"

"Don't you see it?" Mr. Nelson answered, indicating with eyes and gesture the five boys and the two giggling girls, and answering the roguish look in her eyes with a frank laugh. "Don't you know about this enterprise, Miss Bronson?"

"Not in the least, except that a little midget invited me to attend a temperance meeting tonight, and I have come to attend it."

"And you don't find it," laughed Mr. Nelson. "Well, it's in process of manufacture. Let me tell you about it; but first let me ask you, are you in sympathy with it?"

"I don't know," said Dell gravely. "I haven't seen it yet."

He laughed again. "Well, if you reside here, Miss Bronson, you know how completely this village is given over to rum. I have never seen anything like it in a place of its size. I have not been here long, but long enough to get the heartache over some of these scenes I have witnessed. I have a class in the Sunday school, and some little influence over the boys who compose it. I determined to make an effort in the way of a temperance society. I drew up a pledge and got my boys to sign it, and two or three of their sisters signed, then I prepared a pledge for each one, and sent them out after recruits, telling them to invite every one they saw to sign the pledge and attend the temperance meeting this evening. I had some hope of seeing enough present to form a society, and while we all work for temperance, at the same time try to interest the people in a literary effort of some sort."

"And this is the result," said Dell, looking around on eight small people waiting to see what was going to be done with them and, while they waited, whispering together, and giggling simultaneously every few minutes.

"This is the result," Mr. Nelson repeated with becoming gravity, folding his arms and taking a thoughtful survey of his audience and the room in general. Then the two pairs of eyes met and looked at each other for a moment; then the owners of them laughed.

"Small potatoes and a few in a hill," quoted Mr. Nelson feelingly.

"Tall oaks from little acorns grow," responded Dell, ignoring the potatoes. "Mr. Nelson, where is your pastor?"

Mr. Nelson's moustache, and the lip under it, curled very slightly as he answered:

"I have his sympathies, and he hopes I will succeed and be able to do a good work, and he is at Deacon Elliot's playing croquet with Miss Emmeline."

"Oh, he is. What is the reason of all that? I mean, going below surface reasons, why isn't he here?"

"Because, in the first place, Deacon Elliot doesn't approve of temperance societies, thinks pledges an infringement of personal liberty, etc., etc., and Esquire Burton believes in using the good things of this life, as not abusing them, and one of the good things is whiskey; and Mr. Traverse is an unqualified supporter of the antitemperance cause; and these three are the prominent men of the church and the village; and, lastly, our pastor himself thinks good cider is an excellent thing. Have I given you reasons enough?"

"Plenty, and introduced your pastor to me, besides."

"I don't want to slander him," Mr. Nelson said earnestly. "He is a good man. I sincerely believe him to be one, only he thinks on this subject as too many good people do."

Dell's spirits, that had gone down to zero on her entrance into the dreary room, began to rise as difficulties thickened around her.

"Well," she said in a brisk, bright tone, looking with clear, determined eyes into Mr. Nelson's face, "let us have a temperance society, Mr. Nelson, and *succeed*. Will you let me be your coadjutor?"

"I shall be most thankful for any assistance in any form. Under the present highly encouraging circumstances, what would you advise?"

"What was your idea? A literary society?"

"Something of that sort—the two combined, you know."

"Well," spoken with that inimitable little dash of energy, that gave you courage and made you hopeful of results, "let us have a literary society by all means."

"Of what?" said Mr. Nelson with a comical sigh.

"Of the material at hand, to be sure. Little Curly, come here, dear." Thus summoned, the little buff pique morsel came daintily forward from her shy corner by the door, coaxed on by a bright smile and winning gesture from Dell.

"This is the little lady whose pledge I had the honor of signing this morning," she said, as she stooped and placed a protecting arm around the little one.

"Now, my darling, don't you know a nice little verse to say to me; one that you say for papa sometimes, you know?"

"I know 'Jesus loves me,'" the little girl said, with a shy, hesitating voice.

"The very thing! Will you say it for me, darling?"

And the old church was very still; neither whispering nor giggling went on while the sweet child voice was repeating that gem of child poetry:

> Jesus loves me, this I know,
> For the Bible tells me so.

"It is very sweet," Dell said, and her ear had caught that peculiar, clear, round sound, which shows one skilled in such matters; she had found that unusual thing among children, or indeed among those who have long ceased to be children, one who can recite poetry well and naturally.

"It is very sweet indeed. And you said it just as I thought you would. How old are you, little one?"

"I'm almost seven."

"So I thought. Now you will ask Mamma to let you come and see me tomorrow?"

"Mamma is in heaven," the child said, simply and gravely.

"Oh, is she?" And Dell's clasp of the little one tightened. "Do you know my mamma is in heaven too? Perhaps they love each other, your mamma and mine. Well, is your papa here? Can you ask him?"

"Yes." She explained Papa was nearly always in the study, but he let her come in sometimes, when it was *very* necessary, and she could ask him.

"Well, ask him to let you come at four o'clock and stay an hour. I have something very beautiful to teach you." And with a kiss and a smile she was dismissed, while Dell turned triumphantly to Mr. Nelson.

"I have an exquisite piece of poetry to teach her,

and she will recite it beautifully. I knew she would from her eyes. So much is arranged for."

"What next?" asked that gentleman in an amused tone; he seemed suddenly to have slipped into a subordinate position, and left this bright young lady at the head.

"Oh, a declamation we must have next. Mr. Nelson, that lamp nearest you smokes horribly. I don't think you trimmed it very well. I don't think you know quite as much about lamp trimming anyway as you might. Why where is our Tommy True boy? He can speak a piece for us, I think."

She turned to look for him, praised the ingenious arrangements by which he had contrived to make all the windows stay up, contrived by skillful questioning to learn the extent of his oratorical powers, and finally came gleefully back to Mr. Nelson to announce the whole matter successfully arranged. Meantime, his season of utter discouragement having passed, he began to enter with energy and amusement into the preparations, and brought forward the giggling girls to present to Dell. They proved to be young misses of fourteen, who were thoroughly imbued with the spirit of temperance, and quite capable of doing something besides whispering and laughing, if only there could be found people wise enough to set them to work. The election of president, secretary, and the like was by unanimous consent postponed until the next meeting, which was appointed for a week from that evening.

"But what shall we do for an audience?" Mr. Nelson questioned at last in dismay. "We are all performers; where are the listeners?"

"Oh, we'll have listeners," Dell said, with an emphasis that seemed to decide the matter. "In the first place, here are one, two, three—here are ten of us. How many will promise to bring one friend with them next Friday evening, as many more as they can, but one *certainly,* if it is possible?"

Up went her own hand in token of promise. Mr. Nelson promptly took the hint and raised his, and all the others followed their example.

"Then there will be twenty at least. Oh, we'll do very nicely. Ten is not such a poor audience, Mr. Nelson."

"I'm not sure but this is the nicest temperance meeting that I ever attended," she added with a bright laugh. "It's the funniest anyway. See here, Tommy Truman, are you going to be a gentleman and see me home?"

And as Mr. Nelson stood in the doorway of the old church and watched the boy walk proudly down the moonlit street, with the bright lady leaning on his arm, he felt that he would have been perfectly willing to have done that gentlemanly deed himself.

6

THE DRUNKARD'S HOME

I know thy works, and where thou dwellest,
even where Satan's seat is:
and thou holdest fast my name,
and hast not denied my faith.

THEY walked briskly and merrily down the straggling street, until they neared one of the tumbledown shanties, which had a way of appearing right in the midst of more pretentious buildings, looking, by that means, more wildly out of place than they would have done had they been somewhat isolated.

"Dear me!" said Dell in dismay. "What a house! What a place to live in! How should you like to have such a crazy-looking, broken-windowed den as that for a home?"

"I shouldn't like it," Tommy said emphatically.

"Well, between you and me, I don't believe the people who live there like it either in the least. I'll tell you what it is, Tommy Truman; when you get to be a man, and have a family to take care of, if you go and live in such a way that by and by you have to move your family into such a rickety old hovel as that, why I shall be dreadfully disappointed in you."

"I never shall; you may depend," said Tommy, his tones bristling with earnestness and determination.

"I'm glad you are so decided about it," Dell answered approvingly. "Because now you see you will be likely to set about keeping out of such places; set about it right away, I mean. Things don't happen all at once, you see. They begin to get ready away back, years and years before we think about them. I have a fancy that even that old house didn't come into this wretched condition all at once; perhaps there was a time when all the lights were in the windows."

"I know there was," answered Tommy decidedly. "When that old fellow moved in here, there wasn't a pane of glass gone, and things looked kind of decent. I remember the night Sam smashed the first one; he jammed his fist right through it and made it bleed like sixty, too."

Further explanation from Tommy was checked by sounds of banging and scuffling issuing from the said house, and finally a scream, full of mingled terror and anger, checked their footsteps and made Dell's heart, at least, beat faster.

"What can be the matter?" she said anxiously, as they stopped and peered back at the house which they had just passed.

"Oh, Sam is drunk, I suppose," Tommy explained contemptuously. "He is most every night of his life, and he tears around like a madman. He's got a little girl only six years old, and he whips her like all possessed. He'll kill her sometime, folks think."

"He's whipping her now," said Dell as the sounds of blows and screams came out to them distinctly on the evening air. "Tommy, this is dreadful. Can't anything be done? Can't you and I do something, don't you suppose?" and she turned and went with swift steps back to the house.

"Oh, Miss Bronson," Tommy made answer, earnestly, "we can't do anything with him; when he's drunk he is just like a crazy man; folks are afraid to go near him."

Nevertheless he followed her back to the door. Dell had her hand on the latch, and, by way of answering, she said, "Why, it's our Sam. I can see him through the window." Then she pushed open the door and entered.

"Ain't you awful afraid?" asked Tommy, quaking even to the toes of his new boots, yet at the same time aching for an adventure. But Dell addressed her next remark to the crazy man inside. "Why, Sam Miller? Now aren't you ashamed of yourself?"

It does not need picturing the scene that met her eye. It was the same old miserable story that we Americans are so accustomed to and so delight in, that we take few, if any, measures to prevent its daily repetition—a drunkard's home, and whatever of squalid wretchedness and filth are needed to enliven the scene, a drunkard's wife cowering in a corner, alternately weeping and screaming while her husband held by the shoulder with iron grip their youngest child, six years old, and struck blows thick and fast with the round of a chair on the bare neck and arms or yellow head of the shrieking child. Not an unusual picture in the least, you perceive; in fact, only a very commonplace one, lacking in several details that are often added to make it more striking and noticeable. It was not new to Dell, for with her Uncle Edward she had penetrated into all sorts of fearful spots, where people huddled and called themselves at home; for this delightful rum, that so beautifies every picture that it touches, was to be found in Boston as well as in Lewiston.

But there was one feature of it that was new to her

and quite sufficiently striking. It was the first time that she had ever beheld such a picture, having a vivid sense of the fact that her father was the artist entitled to all the honors for the grouping of the scene and the vivid effects that had been produced. Hitherto, Dell, looking upon some poor drunken wretch, had shuddered with horror and mentally expended her bitter, burning indignation on some unknown and terrible villain who had sold the rum. But didn't she know, only too well, where Sam Miller procured his poison? He was a habitual hanger-on at her father's tavern, a regularly engaged help, bringing for her use innumerable pails of water, and papers or anything she chose to send him for in the course of the day, and receiving his payment in rum! What an awful background to the picture before her!

Meantime Sam Miller eyed her glaringly and with dangerous menace at first; and then as there stole over his bewildered senses a dim notion of who she was, a faint memory of the numberless kind words and pleasant smiles that she had bestowed on him, during the last ten days, must have crossed his brain, for the angry glare gave place to a sheepish side glance, and muttering something about the young imp needing a whipping every hour, he abruptly thrust her from him and stumbled rapidly up the rickety stairs, out of sight and sound. Then a curious scene ensued. Dell, having met with unexpected success, turned to comfort the wife, who had caught up her child the moment she was released, and met, to her astonishment, angry eyes and tongue.

"And what kind of manners do you call it, for a fine lady to burst into a man's own house in the night, when he's correcting his girl, and ask him if he ain't ashamed of himself? It's yourself I am thinking might be ashamed, seeing you've no more manners than that."

Dell, taken utterly by surprise, was silent with amazement. Not so with Tommy. He burst forth with fiery indignation:

"Now, Mary Miller, that's a little the meanest thing out. You wanted little Mamie killed out and out, I s'pose? He'd have done it with a few more thumps, and you go and come down on the lady that saved her life!"

A great sob burst from the woman's throat as she went eagerly about ministering to the suffering child; but her voice retained all its bitterness.

"I don't care," she muttered; "them as thrives by the thing that makes a madman of him ain't the ones to ask him if he's ashamed. He ain't himself, Sam ain't. He wouldn't hurt Mamie more'n he would his own self, nor so much, if he knew what he was about. And it's her and hers that's made him what he is. I know who she is, and who her father is, and I hate 'em both. I know how she gets her fine clothes and things; my Sam, and lots of others, gets them for her, and she needn't flaunt them here in my face and tell my Sam to be ashamed of himself. I won't stand it, I won't; so now." And then the hard voice broke down in great bitter tears that seemed wrung from her against her will, each with a groan. Poor Dell! Poor, sad-hearted girl, standing there in her youth and beauty, with her white robes floating snowily around her. What an aching heart they covered! She stood for a moment, after the voice ceased, transfixed by the sting of the hard words, until Tommy's voice roused her.

"Come, Miss Bronson, don't stay where people don't know enough to tell a friend from an enemy."

Then she went swiftly forward to the woman's side and spoke rapidly:

"Mrs. Miller, you ought to put cold water on the child's head, bathe the lumps in ice-cold water, and it will keep them from swelling and relieve the pain. And, Mrs. Miller, you think you know me, but you don't; I hate it, this awful business, this selling poison, with such a hatred as I haven't words to express. I am fighting against it, and praying against it, and I will do so as long as I live." Then she turned and went swiftly away.

They walked along the deserted street in silence, until they neared Dell's home. Tommy broke the stillness.

"Miss Bronson, don't feel bad about what that woman said; she was half crazy, you see, and she don't know anything, anyhow."

Dell smiled drearily and gave her attention to the three or four men who were staggering, and swearing, and whistling along the street, having just issued from her father's hospitable doors, every one of them in different stages of intoxication.

"Oh, Tommy, Tommy," she sighed; "we need a temperance society, don't we?"

"Yes, we do," said sturdy Tommy Truman, true to his principles of strict temperance even then, when he would have liked to comfort her heart with the assurance that nothing of the kind was needed.

Dell replied with solemn eagerness: "Well, Tommy, let us have a temperance society, one that will be worth something; let you and I work for it with all our might and main, in every way that we can think of; let us talk about it wherever we go and with whomever we see; let us think about it constantly, and pray about it a great deal. Will you do it, Tommy?"

And Tommy, standing there in the moonlight, took off his hat and answered with very grave and earnest words:

"Yes, Miss Bronson, I will; just as sure as my name is Tommy Truman, I will do everything I possibly can."

Dell let herself into the dismal house, and paused with a kind of fascinated shudder at the barroom door; the loungers had dropped off into silence and drowsiness earlier than usual, and their deep-snoring breaths, mingled with the sizzling of the kerosene lamp, made the only sounds there were. Tilted back in his armchair, his feet on one of the tables, sat her father, snoring with the rest, the red-bloated face looking more red and more bloated than ever before, and what light there was shone full on his thin hair, singling out from among the black locks many and many a white hair, telling of fast-coming age and swift decay. And he was her father! that bloated, disfigured, disgusting being! She turned and ran with swift steps away from the dreadful sight, up to her own room, and turned the creaking button to fasten herself in. Then she struck a light and, dropping into her little sewing chair, gave herself up to something as near despair as Dell Bronson's healthy, cheery nature ever reached.

"It is all true," she said bitterly; "just as that poor woman said, I am a rum seller's daughter. It must seem to lookers-on as though the very clothes I wear are bought with the price of misery, such as I saw tonight. What can I do? My hands are just completely tied. Uncle Edward doesn't know; if he realized how it was, he would see that I can do nothing. It would be better for me to give up all public attempts, at least. What perfect mockery it must seem to people to have me mixing myself up with a temperance society; and I live in a rum tavern, and my father sells the rum with his own hands, yes, and drinks it too—he is almost as bad tonight as those poor wretches that I met—if he were to try to walk, he would stagger along, just as they did, perhaps. Oh, Father, Father! Oh! Why must I have such a one? There are such good fathers in the world." And then Dell's words broke into sobs, and there came over her a perfect storm of tears.

The weeping lasted but for a few minutes, however; this girl was not much given to crying. After a while she began to move around the room, gathering into their places the things which she had flung from her when she entered, and otherwise tidying the place for the night. During the almost two weeks that she had been at home, she had wrought many changes in the room; the blue paper curtains had given place to full white muslin ones, the bed was spread in white, as also was the little toilet table, and many little feminine, graceful touches had softened its hard corners and given it a look of home. Still there was no sort of comparison between it and that green-and-white room in Boston; and the poor homesick girl's thoughts went on swift wing back to that dear home that had surrounded her life with so much beauty and brightness. She had regained her composure, but her face was sad as, having completed her preparations for the night, she took her little Bible and opened to the mark, for her few verses of evening bread. She was reading in the book of Jeremiah, and yesterday's date was placed after the tenth verse of the twenty-ninth chapter, so the reading commenced:

"For I know the thoughts that I think toward you, saith the Lord, thoughts of peace, and not of evil, to give you an expected end. Then shall ye call upon me, and ye shall go and pray unto me, and I will hearken unto you."

Just there she paused, with a sudden glad light flashing in her eyes and glowing over her face. Could her heart read more than those two verses just then? "And ye shall go and pray unto me, and I will hearken unto you." Was ever anything so marvelous? Why, she had thought herself alone, and desolate and forgotten, and here was the King himself speaking to her, and such words: "For I know the thoughts that I think toward you, saith the Lord." Yes, she had forgotten. She had thought for a little while that the whole weight of this burden rested on her, whereas it was the Lord's affair; he knew all about it, all—all the sorrow, and the discouragement, and the disgrace—and his thoughts were of peace and not of evil. "Then shall ye call upon me." Yes, she would. How could she have yielded to discouragement and tears? She, the daughter of the King! "Ye shall go and pray, and I will hearken unto you." With these words on her lips, Dell sought an audience with her Kingly Father. And the burden of her prayer was "O Father in heaven, remember my poor, tempted, wandering, earthly father; give him to me, in answer to my prayer; and, Father, do save Sam Miller, that poor, miserable man that I saw tonight. Show me how to work for them—help me."

It was a very quiet spirit that Dell carried with her to her rest that night, and the last words that her lips murmured as she dropped into sleep were: "For I know the thoughts that I think toward you, saith the Lord, thoughts of peace, and not of evil, to give you an expected end."

7

The Infant Class

Enter not into the path of the wicked.

DELL BRONSON stood in the cupboard that served as a hall for the dismal church, pretty well squeezed up against the wall to be out of the way of the people, and fanned herself vigorously, waiting for the congregation to pass by, and for what would come next. She looked remarkably pretty standing there, in her Boston-made suit of white lawn, pure and fresh, belted with blue, and a blue sash at her throat. Aunt Laura had been very fastidious as to her darling's appearance, and to Dell it had almost been made to appear a Christian duty to look fresh and neat, and as pretty as she conveniently could. I think it is one. I wish the people who take exception to us, who are on the radical side of the question of dress, did not invariably suppose that because we do gravely and steadily object to the accumulation of silk, and lace, and flounce, and ruffle, and fold, and double plaits, and single plaits, and box plaits, and double box plaits, and fringe, and gimp, and ribbons, and bows, and loops, and masses of jupe, and mohair, and horsehair, and forests of curls, and braids, and frizzes—those things that fashion orders for one poor little suffering body to carry around with her—

that we, therefore, of necessity believe that she must clothe herself in a straight-up-and-down gray gown, and never by any chance wear a bright ribbon or a dainty flower. Why must people be always supposed to run to extremes?

The young people of Lewiston seemed to think that she looked very nice, or very something, for they stared at her in a manner that made her cheeks burn. Some of them said she had altogether too much style on for only a tavern keeper's daughter. In point of fact, she was very simply and inexpensively dressed. There were silks there rustling by her that cost almost as much a yard as her whole suit did, for there were expensive silks worn even in Lewiston, by people who every Sabbath rustled themselves into some forlorn old pew of the dingy church and complacently endured its dinginess. Why shouldn't they? It was not their parlors; it was only a church. But Dell had about her that indescribable air which marks some people of rare good breeding, whether they chance to be clothed in calico or silk, and which those who cannot explain it nor copy it always curl their lips at and call style.

Mr. Nelson came hurriedly over to Dell as she stood in her corner.

"Are you going to remain at Sabbath school, Miss Bronson?"

"Yes," she answered unhesitatingly. It would seem a strange thing for a young lady educated by Mr. Edward Stockwell of Boston not to remain at Sabbath school. This was her first Sabbath at church in Lewiston. The previous Sabbath a sick headache had kept her all day a prisoner, so she was a stranger.

"Well, could you be persuaded to take our infant

class? The teacher is absent, and I know of no one but yourself to take her place."

The infant class! That was not new work to Dell. She had been one of the subteachers in the infant room of the Sabbath school that Uncle Edward superintended. Visions of it rose at once before her—the large, well-lighted, well-ventilated, neatly carpeted room, with its rows and rows of seats arranged tier above tier, all filled with bright baby faces; its desk for the teacher's use, with its large pictorial Bible and pictorial dictionary, the silver call bell, the box of colored crayons, and always, at this season, a dainty vase of sweet-smelling flowers. At the right of the table the handsome reversible blackboard, and charts, and illuminated texts, and maps of Bible lands hanging in rich profusion all along the walls. But today she hesitated. She was not given to hesitation either; her religious education had been "Do with thy might whatsoever thy hand findeth to do"; not that version of later day, "Don't do anything that isn't perfectly agreeable to you in all its details, nor even then unless you happen to feel like it."

"I am not prepared with the lesson, you know. Where is it?"

Mr. Nelson gave his shoulders a peculiarly expressive shrug.

"That need make no sort of difference; no one ever was, I fancy, who has taught that class. The lesson? Why, it's anywhere between the lids of the Bible, or out of it, for that matter, if you happen to think of a story that won't hinge on a Bible verse."

Dell looked aghast. "You don't mean that they have no regular lesson?"

"Aye; I meant just that. Each teacher revels through the realm of fact and fiction at her own sweet will, hinging her thoughts on Bible truth if she can. A wide sphere you see, and if worse comes to worst there is always Moses in the bulrushes, you know, though I can't promise you that they may not be weary of it, as the little girl in the paper was."

"How was that?"

"Have you not seen it? Why, the story goes, that the regular teacher of the class being absent, the substitute was doing Moses in the bulrushes, and in the midst of her recitation one weary little five-year-old raised her fat baby hand, and on being allowed to speak, said, "Oh, please, Miss Jones, I'm jest sick and tired of Moses in the bulrushes!""

Dell laughed softly; most of the congregation were gone now, and they were gathering for the Sunday school. Mr. Nelson, perceiving this, hastened his movements.

"The fact is, Miss Bronson, the infant class is an experiment and is not succeeding very well because of the inefficiency of the teacher; the one who has taken it is never present three Sabbaths in succession, and sometimes I think it would be just as well if she were absent altogether. She doesn't understand the management of an infant class and doesn't interest herself to learn; if you would only take it today?"

"Where is their classroom?"

"Up there."

Dell looked about her and above her, but saw no chance for a classroom.

"Do you mean that hole in the wall?" she asked at last.

Mr. Nelson laughed. "Just about that; it would be a pretty fair description of the room, though there are stairs to reach it by."

"Have you a blackboard?"

"Not a bit of it, nor a chart, nor a picture, nothing but a bare room and some children."

"Without any lesson or any teacher," said Dell, her heart swelling with indignation. "Poor things! Well, I will take the class and do the best that I can for them, and I shall say nothing about Moses in the bulrushes, Mr. Nelson."

So presently he conducted her to the "hole in the wall" and left her there to do what she could. It was a long, narrow, dirty room, with seats that were much too high, so that the rows of little feet dangled, and ambitious toes tried in vain to touch the floor. There were seventeen children, most of them wee ones, all staring curiously at Dell. Among them she recognized her little pique acquaintance, who was made happy and two inches taller by the gift of a special smile and bow.

"What can you sing?" was Dell's first question; and after much circumlocution, it was discovered that while one knew this piece and another that, they could not all unite on anything; they had not been in the habit of singing in the class, and they smiled at the idea as something new and funny. Their teacher immediately commenced teaching them that blessed and world-known child's hymn:

> Jesus loves me, this I know,
> For the Bible tells me so.

And after a fashion they presently sang it and most thoroughly enjoyed doing so. Next, a lesson; and she soon discovered that she was expected to spend the precious half hour in hearing each child blunder through a verse of Scripture that bore not the slightest connection to any other verse recited, and that probably they had repeated several times to some of their numerous teachers. Such was not Dell's idea of Sabbath teaching. She looked about her thoughtfully. She had in mind a lesson prepared for her class in Boston, but to teach that she needed a blackboard. One of the windows had a white curtain, or one that once was white; the other was curtainless, that suggested the idea that the fallen curtain must be somewhere, and after a short search she drew it out from a pile of fallen plaster and other rubbish over in the corner; its condition certainly could not be greatly impaired by the addition of a few pencil marks. So her resolution was swiftly taken, and in less time than it takes us to write it, the curtain was securely fastened by four pins to the wall, doing duty as a blackboard. Meantime every eye was fixed on her in silent and wondering attention. Then she gave them this verse: "Enter not into the path of the wicked." Again and again the seventeen little tongues repeated it, until it seemed firmly fixed. Then she turned to the blackboard and drew two heavy black lines starting together and diverging gradually, being as far apart at last as the limits of the curtain would allow; the line pointing upward was straight and firm, and the lower one was very crooked.

"Now, little folks," she said, speaking with a crisp energy that of itself would waken dormant faculties, "I'm going to tell you a story about Charlie and Johnny. They were brothers—never mind their last name—we will call them Charlie and Johnny. What is our verse? Yes, that little boy in the corner said it just exactly right, 'Enter not into the path of the wicked.' Now this mark, that goes away down to the lower end of the curtain, I have made for a picture of that path of the wicked; you see it goes down, down, and here at the end I will put a large letter *H,* which will stand for the name of the place where this path ends. Who can tell me the dreadful name that we don't like to speak or think of where God said wicked people must go?"

Dell's little girl friend pronounced the awful word in an awe-stricken voice.

"Yes," said Dell. "That is the sad, sad word; we don't like to speak it and need not. God doesn't ask us to speak the dreadful word very often; but we must never forget that there is such a place, and that God said so. Now, all the people who travel this road have a leader, someone who helps them along, and who, when sometimes they want to get away, coaxes them to stay; and beside the letter *H,* I will put the first letter of his name: *S.* Who can tell me what the name is?"

The answer was promptly given.

"And now," said Dell, "let us go up here to the end of the other line; and for the place that the line ends in, I can put another *H,* and all who can may tell me the name of the beautiful city where all the people, who travel on this straight line, will go to someday."

Every eye was fixed on the curtain that was pinned on the wall, and seventeen little tongues shouted out in chorus:

"Heaven!"

"And the name of the leader? For they have a leader on the road, too, and he is much greater and stronger than the other one, and he is always looking out for people who are going on that crooked road down there and urging them to come up to him. His name too commences with *S,* but it is, oh! so different from the other name. I will print the *S* right here by this *H,* and you may tell me the name."

And they were ready, those eager little ones, to speak the name:

"Savior!"

"And now," said Dell, again "for our story about Johnny and Charlie. They were—what relation were they?"

And every one of the seventeen tongues shouted, "Brothers!" in a way that must have astonished the people in the church below. "Yes, they were brothers. Every single one of you remembered; I am glad of that; they both started on their journey up here in this thick line, and for a while they kept pretty close together; they both knew about these two roads, and where they led, and the two leaders; their mother had told them all about it, and of course they thought that they didn't want to travel down on the crooked road with such a dreadful leader, and they almost made up their mind that they wouldn't. Boys always do; I never saw a boy or girl in my life who really wanted to go on the crooked road. They every one almost make up their minds not to—they don't quite decide it though, for if they did they would be safe; nobody can possibly make them go on that road if they are quite determined not to. These two boys walked along together, very near the straight line you see, not on it, because they were not quite decided; but they thought they were, and they meant to be very good, and sometimes they tried; they said their prayers at night, and they tried to obey their mother during the day, and you see how it was by this line that I am drawing, they almost go on the straight road. One day some wicked boys asked them to run away from school, coaxed them, and after a while don't you think they both decided to go, and then you see where they went, right down toward the crooked line as fast as they could." And with her pencil Dell turned the course of their lives downward. "But Charlie felt very sorry that he had started, and soon he began to coax Johnny to turn back, and Johnny wouldn't; so, after a little, Charlie left him and went up this way, toward the straight line; he told his mother how he had been tempted and almost gone into the wicked path, and he asked the Savior to forgive him, and he almost decided to go up into the straight path and take the Savior for his guide; but he was not quite decided yet, so he stayed below, so near, you see, that he almost touched the straight line. But poor Johnny! Here he is down here; he had entered the path of the wicked. I wish I had time to tell you of all the sad things that happened to him. I'll tell you of one. Down here where I make this mark, there was a place where they sold rum, and there Johnny got in the habit of going; he bought the liquor and drank it; he began to like the taste of it very much."

Just at this point an excited little fellow in the corner called out:

"Was it down to this tavern on the corner where he went?"

Poor Dell! Her own home brought forward to point her story. Her cheeks were very red, but she answered, steadily:

"No, that was not the place, but it was just like that place, and that tavern will do just as much harm to those that are coaxed into it, as this one did that I am telling you of. Sometimes Johnny felt very sorry that he had entered into this wicked path, and once or twice he made up his mind to come out of it, and he got out—here is the line to show where he went; he stopped drinking rum, and he tried to do some right things, and you see he went up toward the straight line but not into it, because he couldn't quite make up his mind to ask the Savior to lead him; if he had he would have been safe; but the wicked people came after him, and Satan tried to get him to go back to that place and drink more rum; and so one day he went down, down, right into that place again, and he kept on going there and doing a great many wicked things; and one day when he had been drinking a great deal they turned him out into the street, and he lay in the gutter all night, and in the morning he was dead!" And Dell's pencil and line pointed in solemn silence right at the edge of that fearful letter *H;* and the children, awed and impressed as probably they had never been in their lives before, looked and were silent.

"It was about that time," continued Dell at last, when she could command her voice, "that Charlie began to try harder than ever to get into the straight road, and yet he didn't try in quite the right way; he didn't ask the Savior to lead him; he would keep quite near the straight road for a whole day, and then he would do something wrong and go away down like this; but one day after he was almost discouraged in trying to help himself, the Savior kept whispering, 'Come to me; I will help you,' and after thinking it all over he quite decided to go, and that very hour he went up this way." And as Dell's pencil touched the firm straight line, her little friend, who had been growing more eager and interested every moment, suddenly broke the stillness by exclaiming, "He's in! He's in! Oh, I am so glad."

The bell rang below, and Dell's half hour was gone; she had done her best, with what result, God knew.

8

FINDING RECRUITS FOR THE TEMPERANCE ARMY

The steps of a good man are ordered by the Lord.

THE cracked bell in the old church steeple clanged faithfully on that Friday evening. Dell attended to the matter; she went herself to the sexton and coaxed him into promising to ring it for just ten minutes. She stood in the hall all ready with one exception. She had failed to secure the promised "one anyway," as a surety of an audience. She had tried several persons, but they all with one accord began to make excuse. As she stood leaning against the doorway, wondering if there was not another last effort that she could make somewhere, a bright thought came to her. Sam Miller was at that moment sawing wood out in the wood yard; she could hear the lazy motion of his saw scraping back and forth. She could ask him. Of course it was more than likely that he wouldn't go; but it could do no harm to try; she ran out to him.

"Sam," she said, gathering up her dainty dress and posing herself on an unsawn stick of wood, "I've come after you. I want you to go to the temperance meeting with me tonight; will you?"

Sam looked first aghast, then amused.

"Why," he said, "I can't go to them sort of things; it ain't no use. It ain't of any account."

"Go and try one. I don't believe you have ever been. We are going to have singing. I know you are fond of music. I heard you singing 'Molly Bawn' this morning. I like your voice. I want you to come and help us sing."

Sam leaned on his saw meditatively.

"You'd be wanting me to sign the pledge now, I dare say, if I went there?" he said inquiringly, with a cunning look in his eyes.

"Why, of course, I should invite you to do so. Are you so afraid of a pledge that you don't even dare to meet one face to face for a few minutes? You won't be made to sign it, you know, if you don't choose to do so."

Sam's voice took a plaintive turn.

"It ain't no good for me to have to do with them kind of things, Miss Bronson. It ain't truly. I'm nothing but an old loafer now days, and I know it, and I keep away from nice folks. I'm all gone to wreck and ruin; ain't worth taking any notice of."

Dell stooped and picked up a chip and broke it into little bits while she talked.

"You don't mean a word of that, Sam, not a single word of it; if anyone should say it to you, you would be angry enough to choke them. You know you are worth a good deal, and now and then when you look at little Mamie, you think that you'll never drink another drop of that horrid rum; and that you will work hard so that Mamie can have nice things to wear, and go to school, and have as good a chance as any girl of her age."

She had tried him at a venture and had touched the

tender spot in his heart; he put up his rough, hard hand and brushed it across his eyes.

"That's true," he said at last. "True as preaching; sometimes I think I'll manage somehow to give her a chance. But then, you see, it's no kind of use. I can't do it. I've tried, and tried, and made promises by the bushel, and it never did the least mite of good. I've got to drink."

There was a genuine plaintiveness in his voice this time, and Dell felt that it was time to turn comforter.

"You've never tried the help that the pledge would give you," she said cheerily. "Suppose you make a grand start, sign the pledge, and that of itself will give you strength, and then temperance people will know that you are trying, and we will all help you."

But Sam Miller was not to be so easily won. He really wanted to reform; that is, now and then he did, when he thought of Mamie; but the wish was very weak and wouldn't bear the test of a stern, strong effort. He turned from Dell and took his saw again with a mournful shake of the head.

"I can't do that. I know I wouldn't keep it, and where would be the use? I'd be worse off than I was before I tried."

Dell decided to waive that part of the subject.

"I have a very special reason for wanting you to go to the meeting with me tonight," she said eagerly. "You see, we each promised last week that we would bring someone with us this evening, and now if you fail me, I shall have to go alone, and I don't like to at all."

Sam Miller turned halfway round again from his stick of wood and laid down his saw. This was evidently a new phase of the question. The bright young creature before him had not been bestowing smiles and kindly words on him all the week for nothing.

"Why, if it would be a kind of an accommodation like," he said, speaking slowly and in much embarrassment, "why, I suppose I could go."

"It would be a real accommodation. I want to keep my promise, you know."

"But you won't ask me to sign one of them pledges, will you?"

"I'll ask you to, certainly, if I get a chance; but of course no one will compel you to sign it, if you really make up your mind that you won't."

Sam meditated still further.

"Well," he said at last, "you go on, and tell 'em your someone is coming. I'll come along down that way by and by, I guess."

"Oh, no," said Dell persuasively. She was very fearful of the attractions of the barroom that he would be likely to pass through. "That wouldn't be bringing someone with me; that's what I promised. I want you to walk down the street and into the church with me."

"Well," said Sam again, giving the stick of wood an emphatic kick, and speaking with energy and decision, as if he had conquered an invisible foe. "I'll go now; I'll be hanged if I won't."

And he went. He shambled through the one long street by the side of the dainty, well-dressed young lady, and more than one lounger at the village stores looked after them with curious eyes. The bell had ceased its clanging, and there was quite a little company gathered inside the church. Much pains had been taken to spread the news of the meeting, and curiosity had drawn in several who were not deeply interested in the cause.

"There's forty-four folks in the church this very minute," Tommy Truman announced in a very loud and very gleeful whisper to Dell as she entered the door.

"There are! Isn't that splendid?" the young lady responded in a voice not so loud, but every bit as gleeful.

Then Mr. Nelson made his way toward her.

"Are the lamps better?" he asked gravely. "Haven't I improved in the art of cleaning and trimming them? Shall we open this remarkable meeting with a song, if we can get anybody to sing it?"

"A great deal brighter, Mr. Nelson; the church really looks almost cheerful. I should think it would be better to open with prayer."

The seriocomic look on Mr. Nelson's face faded into one of perplexed gravity.

"Why, should you?" he asked in a grave and troubled tone.

"Why, I don't suppose it makes much difference which way it is," Dell said cheerily. "It only struck me as the most appropriate way. Would you prefer to sing first?"

"I—I had not thought it necessary to have prayer at all," he said hesitatingly.

It was Dell's turn to look grave and surprised.

"I confess," she said, speaking with quiet dignity, "that to me it seems almost, if not quite, a necessity."

"There is no one here to call on," giving a swift glance around the room.

"Can't you call on yourself, Mr. Nelson?"

"Not very well; I'm not in the habit of it."

"Of praying in public do you mean?"

"Yes, or in private either," he answered her quickly, with a slightly embarrassed laugh. "I don't wish to dress in sheep's clothing, Miss Bronson. I see you have mistaken my character."

Dell was silent from utter surprise and disappointment. But Mr. Nelson almost immediately added in a relieved tone, "Oh, we are all right after all; here comes Mr. Tresevant, and he has Miss Emmeline Elliot with him. I think she will play for us." And while he hastened to meet the minister, Dell slid quietly into a seat, still wearing her grave face; it had been a great disappointment; she had thought she had recognized one of the children of the King.

Mr. Tresevant immediately went forward and offered a very fervent prayer. To be sure he did not say the word *temperance,* but he slid around it and glided almost up to it in that dexterous way that some good and skillful people have a habit of doing, who do not quite like to give a square utterance to the obnoxious word. After the prayer a great whispering ensued. Miss Emmeline Elliot was being coaxed to play. And she looked smiling and accommodating and persistently shook her head. She had not thought of such a thing. She only came in for a little while as a spectator. She could not think of taking any part in the exercises. She hated to play on a cabinet organ anyway and was not at all accustomed to it, Mr. Nelson knew, and that one was horridly out of tune; it made her teeth ache even to hear it, and, well, he really must excuse her. A timid girl in the corner was petitioned; she grew red from chin to forehead at the bare thought and looked so thoroughly frightened that Mr. Nelson did not wait for the refusal. Several others were tried with like results, Dell meantime looking on, half amused and half provoked.

What a time! she said to herself. *Now why can't that man ask me to play? What is the use of his taking for granted that I can't do anything? I've a mind to offer my services. I won't either. He might at least venture the inquiry; it wouldn't take long. Let him go without music if he can't invite me. Now, Dell Bronson, that's a charming way to do; your Uncle Edward would be proud of his pupil, wouldn't he?*

The end of it was that she telegraphed Tommy Truman with her eye and sent him after Mr. Nelson. When he came, looking greatly perplexed and saying, "I don't see but we shall have to do without music after all," she answered:

"If you would give me an invitation, how do you know but I would play for you?"

"You?" he said, with brightening face. "Can you?"

"I can try," she answered demurely, and without further delay she went forward to the instrument. She laughed a little inwardly at her position. It so happened that so far as being musician was concerned, the position was not at all novel. Even in cultured, musical Boston, her playing and her voice were decidedly noticeable; and here were these people staring at her as though they could not recover from their surprise. Mr. Nelson brought her the old notebook and selected the piece he wished to sing.

"Shall I read it?" Dell questioned. And again he answered, "If you can." And then her fingers swept the keys. It was a different touch from that to which the wheezy old organ was accustomed, and it rolled forth grandly in honor of its player; and when Dell's rich, full, cultured voice filled the room, the squeak and the wheezing were alike forgotten. Lewiston had a surprise. Miss Emmeline Elliot straightened herself, let her lace shawl droop gracefully or otherwise as it pleased, and listened intently, discovering, while she listened, that she was no longer *the* player of Lewiston; that Dell Bronson, the tavern keeper's daughter, could draw from those disordered keys such music as she had scarcely ever dreamed of. The church windows and doors were wide open, and as the new, powerful voice was rolled out, passers-by halted at the gate, listened, and by twos and threes strolled in.

"Sing twenty verses, and for once in its life the church will be full," whispered Mr. Nelson in one of the interludes, as he bent with shining eyes to turn the leaves. And Dell, singing on, just gloried in the power that God had given her, the power of song; though she had sung so much, she had never realized the joy of her voice, the use to which it might be put, as she did that night.

That temperance meeting was a grand success; there was much singing, Dell was not sparing of her voice, and it fulfilled its mission well. People gathered in, so that when dainty little Lora Tresevant, Dell's pique acquaintance, came forward in her freshest white dress to recite her piece, she was half frightened at the rows of eyes gazing at her. She had been carefully trained, and her soft little voice was clear and sweet as she commenced that most exquisite of child poems:

> *There's no rain left in the heaven!*
> *There's no dew left on the daisies and clover,*
> *I've said my seven times over and over,*
> *Seven times one are seven.*
>
> *I am old, so old, I can write a letter;*
> *My birthday lessons are done;*
> *The lambs play always, they know no better;*
> *They are only one times one.*
>
> *O moon! in the night I have seen you sailing*
> *And shining so bright and low;*
> *You were bright! ah, bright! but your light is failing,*
> *You are nothing now but a bow.*

You moon, have you done something wrong in
   heaven
That God hath hidden your face?
I hope if you have you'll soon be forgiven,
And shine again in your place.

O velvet bee, you're a dusty fellow,
You've powdered your legs with gold!
O brave marsh marybuds, rich and yellow,
Give me your money to hold.

O columbine, open your folded wrapper,
Where two twin turtle doves dwell!
O cuckoopint, toll me the purple clapper,
That hangs in your clear green bell!
And show me your nest with the young ones in it
I am old, you may trust me, linnet, linnet,
I am seven times old today.

Tommy Truman did himself and his author credit. His round little voice rang clear and strong, and indignantly, over the wrongs and woes of a drunkard's wife. Mr. Nelson made a strong, stirring little speech, and then the singing swelled forth again. They stood together after the meeting, Mr. Nelson, Mr. Tresevant, Miss Elliot, and Dell. Mr. Tresevant was expressing himself neatly and kindly concerning the success of the meeting and the superiority of the music.

"You have really given us a delightful surprise, Miss Bronson"; and Miss Elliot chimed in:

"Yes, indeed. I wasn't aware that you played or sang. You really sing remarkably well."

Dell's eyes danced; she had heard comments on her music before, some of them quite equal to this one.

"I wish I could have been surprised," she said, turning to Mr. Nelson. "I was in hopes that Sam

Miller would surprise me by signing the pledge, but no such good fortune awaited me. Now, if I had been a girl in a book, how promptly he would have signed the pledge, and been a reformed man from this very hour, but being out of a book, and in a most matter-of-fact little town, I suppose I must bide my time. By the way, Mr. Tresevant, I don't see your name here?"

"No," Mr. Tresevant said, flushing slightly, "I am not in a book either and must, therefore, study my steps carefully."

9

THE TEA PARTY

I will make you fishers of men.

THERE'LL be a high old time tonight, Miss Dell, I just expect. I don't look for nothing else." Sally volunteered this information as she cleared off the dinner table.

Dell turned from the window, where she had been overseeing some of Katy's operations, and gave Sally the benefit of a bright smile as she questioned:

"What kind of a time is that, Sally?"

"Why, there's a barn raising up in the hollow, and the folks will be coming home about dark, and the way they'll pour in here won't be slow, and they smokes and drinks most generally them times till twelve o'clock, and sometimes they gets pretty merry."

Dell's smile had vanished, and her eyes had an indignant flash. "I thought they had those disgraceful scenes in the barn after it was raised, and at the expense of the owner?"

"So they does, the workers, but these fellows that come in here are the hangers-on like, who don't do no work and can't get in at the supper, so you see they comes here."

74

The face over by the window was turned suddenly away from Sally, and the fair, brown head drooped low. This was bitter truth to which she had been listening. Her father's guests were those who were not sufficiently respectable to be admitted to the regular merry makings, and so took refuge with him! There were times when those disgraceful truths surged over Dell with such overwhelming power that it seemed to her she must sink beneath them. She struggled against this feeling now. She battled with her hot, indignant tears—they should not fall; they could do no good; she was put here for work, not for weeping. But what to do? Suddenly she turned again to Sally.

"Who told you about all this?"

Sally tossed her head contemptuously.

"Oh, Sam Miller did. He knows everything that's a-going on, and more too. If there's a thing in Lewiston that that fellow don't know about unless it's his own business, I'd like to hear what it is."

Dell left her abruptly to search for Sam. He was in the barroom, and for a wonder it had no other occupant. She leaned coaxingly over the dirty counter.

"Sam, does father know about the raising this afternoon?"

Sam stared. "Not as I knows on," he said at last. "No, I guess he don't; there hain't been a soul in that's spoke of it, as I've heard. He never goes, Miss Bronson." This last was in a tone intended to be encouraging.

"Well, now," said Dell, in confidential tones, "I want Father all to myself this evening. Don't tell him anything about the raising, and if I succeed in getting him to come with me, can't you attend to things here, and not let him be called whoever comes? And, Sam, won't you keep things quiet out here for *me?*"

Sam looked at her solemnly. The poor drunkard understood her object as plainly as though she had expressed it in words and felt a pitiful kind of sympathy for her struggles after her father. He even thought, in a weak, childish sort of way, that if she or somebody were struggling after him in that eager fashion he would give up the rum for her sake. Meantime, of course, he forgot the struggling wife at home and little Mamie.

"I'll do it, if I can," he said impressively. "I'll do the very best I can, but I don't know how much it will be."

"I'll trust you," said Dell, with a peculiar earnestness in her tone, and then she vanished. Her father was in the garden hoeing; thither she followed him and promptly introduced her subject.

"Father, I am going to have a tea party this afternoon; will you come?"

"Not I," he answered emphatically. "Have your tea parties and welcome, child, I'm glad to see you gay; I ain't stingy; you're welcome to all the good things you want, but don't expect me to come to 'em."

"Ah, but I do." And Dell leaned both hands on his arm in a coaxing, winning fashion that reminded him, in spite of himself, of the days when he was young, and Dell's mother clung to his arm.

"I depend on you. I have my plans all made, and you will spoil them all if you don't come, for you see, there is not to be another living being there but you and me."

Her father stared at her in a blank surprise for a few minutes; then he leaned over his hoe and chuckled.

"You're a queer fish," he said at last. "Now what

notion will you take next, I wonder? I'll be blamed if you ever took one like anybody else since you was born."

"Will you come?" Dell repeated with pretty persistency. "I am going to have just such things as you like best for supper, and I shall have the tearoom all brightened up beautifully, so much pleasanter than that long table, and I never sit down with you there, you know. Will you promise?"

Mr. Bronson shook his head. "I can't, child. I've got to eat my supper with the folks; they're good enough for me, and you might sit down with us if you would. It wouldn't look well to see me away from my own table."

"Can't you be invited out to tea once in a while as well as anybody else? I tell you it is my tea party, and, Father, don't you remember how you and Mother and I used to have tea together all alone, once in a while, when I was a little bit of a girl? Oh, Father, I have not had you all to myself once since I came home, and I want it so much; won't you come?"

It is a mistake to suppose that a rum seller has no heart; they are hard to reach, it is true; and I doubt if Jonas Bronson was sure that he had one until Dell's pleading set it into unusual motion. He looked down almost tenderly on the earnest, young face.

"Well," he said at last, "it's as silly a piece of business as ever I heard of; but land's sake, if it will do you any good, I might as well eat my supper in that room for once as t'other one, so if I get back in time, I'll come."

"Oh, are you going away?" she asked, with dismayed face and beating heart. What if he should be going to drop in at the raising after all?

"Got to go to the Corners this afternoon to see Jim

Turner on business, and I declare for it, I ought to be off this minute."

The bright look returned. "Oh, you'll get back," she said gaily; "I know you will, you wouldn't disappoint me for all the Jim Turners in creation; I know you won't."

It is a wonderful thing sometimes to trust a man. Perhaps after all it was more that last sentence than anything else that made Mr. Bronson actually hasten his movements and so drive up to his house ten minutes before six. Meantime Dell had not been idle; the tearoom was a marvel of freshness and beauty; there were flowers and mosses, and also a most daintily spread tea table. Muffins, made by Dell's own hand, such as Sally might have tried in vain to manufacture. She stood looking at it all when the work was done, with a pleased face. She did not expect her father to notice the flowers and mosses; even if he did, he would be likely to call them trumpery, but she had a fancy that the general effect of grace and beauty might linger in his memory as a pleasant thing.

She was on the watch, and ran to the door at the first sound of the wheels, and presently carried her father in gleeful triumph to the tearoom and seated him in the great armchair, with a fresh newspaper in hand, while she went to her muffins. It was a queer little supper; the father and daughter, sitting opposite each other at that round table, had not apparently a single idea in common. The father seemed to feel it most, and it tinged his manner with embarrassment; but Dell exerted herself to talk and laugh and wait on him; and the muffins and cold chicken he certainly enjoyed, likewise the pickled lobster, sent from Boston on purpose for him, Dell informed him.

"You're a good cook," he said complacently, as he

finished his fourth cup of tea and arose from the table. "And a good girl, I guess. I reckon they hain't spoilt you in Boston, for all they tried. Anyhow things are different about the house; you needn't think I don't notice things, 'cause I do. I know when a bed is made comfortable and when it ain't as well as the next man. Your mother was a master hand at making a bed, and you've took after her."

Dell had made her father's room over in every imaginable respect since her return home, and now had it under her daily supervision, so that from being the dingiest and most ill-kept room in the house, it had grown into one that was always fresh and cheery. This was the first time her father had by word or look evinced any knowledge of the change. It was something to know that he appreciated his bed.

She sprang up eagerly; he was looking around for his hat.

"Oh, Father, read the newspaper a few minutes while I get rid of this table, and then I have got something to show you. Here is a Boston daily, which came just a few minutes ago."

"I don't know about it," he said doubtfully. "I guess I ought to go." Nevertheless he took the paper and sat down, while Dell almost breathlessly hurried the dishes out to Katy. Every nerve was on the alert; there was a drawn battle between the tearoom and the barroom that evening, and the daughter knew only too well what a powerful ally that barroom possessed. She came in with a small square board filled with pegs, and watching her chance as the paper began to be turned restlessly, she produced it.

"Father, are you as sharp at puzzles as you used to be? Do you remember those you used to get out for mother? Here is one that I have looked at a great many times, and I don't get it at all."

"Oh, I don't fuss at such nonsense now," he said loftily. "I used to amuse your mother in that way once in a while; and so you remember it, do you? That's queer now; you was just a little mite of a child."

"I wish you would help me with this," Dell said, bending over it with a perplexed face. "I can't see through this in the least, and it provokes me to fail in anything."

Whereupon the father chuckled admiringly. "It does, eh! You're a chip off the old block. I've seen the time that I've bothered for hours over the things, and I always beat 'em, too. Let's see this one."

Never, surely, was the game of solitaire so closely and eagerly watched. Dell bent over the board with glowing cheeks and shining eyes, having in her heart the eager hope not that he would succeed, but that he would fail again and again; for this once accomplished, what could she do next? There seemed little fear of its being accomplished; apparently he had found something that would beat him; he knitted his brows, and pulled out the pegs and stuck them in every imaginable way, and finally threw it down with an impatient "Pshaw! The thing is a humbug; there can't nobody do it."

"How provoking," Dell said innocently. "Professor Thompson can do it in a twinkling; I've seen him; but he does it so fast, you can't tell anything about it. Uncle Edward and I have sat and looked right at him, and then tried, and we couldn't get it."

"Your Uncle Edward can't get it, eh! with all his book learning; that's a smart notion," and he drew it toward him again, and presently the wrinkles came in his forehead, and he was again absorbed.

Dell looked about her for a fan, and fanned hard and fast; she trembled visibly, she had been so frightened lest the puzzle had failed her. There came a low tap at the side door; she arose and opened it softly; it was Sally, respectful and sympathetic, perfectly comprehending what her young mistress was about. She spoke in whispers. "Mr. Elliot and Mr. Nelson are waiting in the parlor to see you, Miss Dell."

Dell did not hesitate for an instant. "Tell them I am very much engaged, and they must excuse me this evening; and, Sally, if anyone else should call, just excuse me without coming."

Slowly but surely the evening waned, and still the puzzle held sway; they held conversation over it now and then; her father called it "the confoundest thing that had ever got hold of him" and slammed it down on the table several times, and as often some innocent remark of Dell's about Uncle Edward's trials over it would give him a fresh impulse. Suddenly a prolonged and triumphant A-ha! announced a victory. He had accomplished the feat; but even then Dell had to be taught, and she proved a stupid pupil, and when she finally felt that it would be wise to learn, her father immediately said:

"There! You've got it. Now I must go. I don't know what that Sam may be about. That lobster of yours must have been uncommon salty; I'm as dry as a fish."

Dell sprang up eagerly. "Oh, are you? How glad I am; I have been hoping you would say so. Now, I'm going to give you a splendid surprise; you think, I suppose, that Sally knows how to make coffee, but you wait just a minute, and see what you think of mine."

There was a low call to Sally, who seemed to be in waiting, a few hurried words with her, and in a very few moments thereafter her father was drinking a cup of very strong, very richly sugared, very thickly creamed coffee—precisely what he liked.

"It is good, that's a fact," he said as he poured it down; the little coffeepot was on hand, and Dell hastened to replenish his cup. As she gave it to him she asked:

"Do you like singing as much as you used to, Father? You have not heard me since I came home. I know that old ballad that Mother used to sing. I'm going to sing it for you." And immediately her full, rich voice filled the room; her father drank his coffee more slowly and presently set down his cup, got out his handkerchief, and blew his nose; there were more memories woven around that song than his daughter knew of. He said not a word when it was finished; indeed she hardly gave him a chance, but warbled off into another old song; he listened certainly, and that was a great deal. Song after song was finished and another commenced, and still he sat silent and attentive; presently his head began to droop, he gave several emphatic nods, and finally settled back against the wall and snored. Dell sang on softly, not daring to stop at first, but soon the snoring became so positive and well defined that she ceased her music; but she stirred neither hand nor foot, she almost wanted to stop breathing. If this blind nap would only wear out the rest of the evening! And so, silent and motionless, she sat through her vigil; the clock from the distant kitchen struck faintly; she tried to count—could it be possible that it was ten o'clock! She drew her tiny watch. Yes—victory! The evening was gone. With a reassuring look at the sleeper, she stole softly from the room across the dining room and hall and peeped into the barroom from the half-open door. It was unusually quiet there; a few loungers were in different stages of drunkenness and sleep; the half-filled, badly trimmed lamps cast their smoky light over the miserable scene; it was no part of Dell's intention to make the barroom inviting, so she left it to uninterrupted dirt and gloom. Sam Miller caught a glimpse of her and came out, speaking earnestly.

"I've kept things just as still as I could. There came a lot of fellows about an hour ago and made a great row and wanted to see your father, but I told him he was out to tea and could not be seen, and pretty soon they went off."

Dell looked at him gratefully. "I know you have kept it very still, and I thank you. Now, Sam, can't you have these people go away, and put out the lights? It's time, I'm sure, and I don't want Father to come here tonight."

"Yes," Sam said virtuously. "It is time, that's a fact. Oh, yes, I can manage that for you. I'll send them home." Which he did most unceremoniously.

"Here, you, Dick Johnson, go and sleep on your own floor; you can't have ours any longer. Jim Cole, get up and go home." And in less than fifteen minutes, each sleepy loafer had staggered off, and the barroom lights were out. Dell went swiftly back to her father; he might waken now whenever he chose. A few minutes more, and then a more decided snore than usual aroused him. He looked around with a bewildered air, remarked that he guessed he had been asleep, then he yawned and stretched himself, and finally drawing his great watch, said:

"Well, I swan! If it ain't going on to eleven o'clock! Why, what the dickens has been going on in the barroom, I wonder."

"It's all right, Father," Dell said cheerily. "Sam has

closed things up and gone home; I told him you were tired, and I thought you wouldn't be out."

"The mischief," he said, staring. "This is a funny evening, I declare. Well, I am tired, that's a fact. Give me another drink of your coffee, and then I'll go to bed."

The door closed on him at last, and Dell sat down with a weary sigh on the couch; the energy was gone; she was tired. A funny evening! Well, it had certainly been a strange one. How hard she had worked, and after all what had she accomplished? It was only one evening. She felt like a feather trying to beat back the waves of the ocean. Would she ever be able to stem the awful tide that was setting against her? She drew the large Bible to her, that she had placed conspicuously on the little table, and wearily turned the leaves, until pausing over the story of the weary fishermen, who had toiled all night and taken nothing, she read the story through; someway it gave her courage. "Nevertheless at thy command, we will let down the net." There was another verse: "Follow me, and I will make you fishers of men." Was not the message to her? Fishers of men. Wasn't she willing to do the work? What if she did toil all night and take nothing— nevertheless at his command. Who could tell what the fruits of that one evening might be? Couldn't God use her toiling? Wasn't it something to have charmed her father into a quiet evening instead of leaving him to a drunken revel? Yes, she would toil not only all night but many nights. Wasn't there always before her the promise, "I will make you fishers of men"? With this to plead, the Elder Brother's own words, could she ever weary over the toiling?

10

DELL'S VISITORS

*I know thy works, that thou art
neither cold nor hot.*

MR. CHESTER ELLIOT and the reverend Mr. Tresevant selected the same evening in which to call on
Dell. It was not by any means Mr. Elliot's first call; he
had seemed anxious to atone for the neglect of his
sister, and had been very cordial and courteous in his
attentions. The talk had been on general topics and
had been decidedly enjoyable, until a slight pause
occurred, when Dell suddenly turned to Mr. Elliot.

"By the way, we are in need of your assistance, Mr.
Elliot; why don't you join our temperance society?"

He laughed good-humoredly and answered care-
lessly:

"I am afraid you wouldn't admit me."

"We certainly would, and be glad to do so. We only
ask you to sign the total abstinence pledge; that con-
stitutes membership."

"Whether it is kept or not, Miss Bronson?" said Mr.
Tresevant.

Something peculiar in the minister's voice or manner annoyed Dell, and she answered, with a height-
ened color and some haughtiness:

"Of course we believe that our members sign in good faith, with intent to keep their promises."

"Which, nevertheless, and unfortunately, sometimes they fail to do. What then?"

"Then happens just what happens in other matters when people fail to keep their promises; they lower themselves in their own estimation and in that of others."

"And do you consider a man better or worse, because of a broken pledge?"

Dell's eyes flashed. "Do you consider a man better or worse, who pledges himself to the church of Christ and then, as unfortunately many do, breaks his pledge?"

"Worse, decidedly," Mr. Tresevant answered composedly.

"And do you, therefore, try to deter a man from uniting with the church lest he may sometime in the future break his promises?"

Mr. Tresevant fidgeted a little in his chair and toyed with the top of his cane.

"I do not, of course," he said at last. "But I need not remind you, Miss Bronson, that the cases are not parallel; that when a person desires to unite with the church, we trust he leans upon the Divine Arm for strength, and there is therefore little danger of his falling. Whereas in the matter of a total abstinence pledge, it is merely a compact between man and his own weak will."

"I didn't know it," Dell answered gravely. "I supposed that every attempt on our part to do right was an evidence of the guiding of the Divine Arm. I imagined that our own weak wills, left to themselves, did not so much as conceive of a right desire."

Mr. Elliot turned with a half-amused, half-earnest air toward his pastor.

"That is the theology that you preach, is it not, sir?" he asked respectfully.

"In general terms, yes," Mr. Tresevant answered, smiling, "but Miss Bronson has very naturally confused the two points."

"I don't in the least understand what you mean," Dell said frankly. "But I just want to say that I have a higher opinion even of our weak human wills than you seem to have. If Mr. Elliot should promise to pay me a certain sum of money on a certain day, and should sign a note to that effect, I must say I should be inclined to think he would do it; but I didn't mean to open a discussion on temperance, but only to ask why he didn't join our society."

"Now, I thought we had thrown you off your track," said that gentleman gaily. "And, behold, here you are at the very same station. Well, the truth is, if I must confess it, I don't think I am prepared to keep the pledge. I should have no objections to signing it if I thought it at all probable that I should keep it for twenty-four hours."

"I am sorry you have so little confidence in your own strength of purpose," Dell said dryly.

"No, you mistake; it is not strength of purpose that is needed, but inclination. You see, I have never been converted to the theory of total abstinence."

"Oh," Dell said very coldly. "If you had the misfortune to live where I do, you would be a speedy convert, I fancy; and I should suppose that one day spent at your father's factory would be likely to have the same effect."

"That is just the point on which we should differ. If you temperance reformers would confine your efforts to the lower classes, I should be with you heartily, and I think you might do a vast deal of good; but I cannot see the use of fettering the world because a few poor wretches abuse their privilege."

Dell's lip curled just a little, and she spoke rapidly:

"Do you believe what you are saying, Mr. Elliot? How long do you suppose it would be necessary for you to talk temperance according to your fashion to Pat Hughes, for instance? I believe he is one of your father's men. Suppose you try it; tell him liquor is a very improper article for him to use; that he belongs to the lower classes, and, therefore, cannot control his appetite, and that he ought by all means to sign the pledge; but that you, being made of different dust from himself, shall continue the moderate use of liquor; when would you expect to see him a reformed man?"

Mr. Elliot shrugged his handsome shoulders. "I shall expect the millennium to come before even you can reform poor Pat, with any sort of temperance effort whatever; but I don't have to carry Pat's conscience, you know. It is enough for me to look after my own."

"Oh! then it resolves itself into the old argument, 'Am I my brother's keeper?' The Christian standpoint would be that you were bound to make every effort in your power to give up every possible indulgence that might stand in his way, to see if by so doing you could not save one soul, made even of such common clay as Pat Hughes."

The flush on Mr. Elliot's cheek deepened slightly, but he answered courteously and with a strong attempt at playfulness:

"Now, you are rather hard on me, Miss Bronson, to lay Pat's failings at my door. Why, he was a drunkard before I was born; but I don't think I stand alone in the matter. Here is Mr. Tresevant; you will admit that he views things from a Christian standpoint; now if you can prevail on him to sign the pledge, I will put my name under his."

Mr. Tresevant nestled uneasily and looked annoyed.

"Miss Bronson and I should differ as to the ways and means, rather than as to the sin of drunkenness," he said quietly. "Of course, if I were convinced that the total abstinence pledge was the best way of meeting this important question, I would sign it without hesitation."

"Perhaps I don't think it the best way myself," Dell answered promptly. "But since it is one of the ways, and one of the best that we have at present, why not use it as far as it goes?"

"But you don't approve of total abstinence pledges at all, do you, sir? I have heard so at least." Mr. Elliot spoke eagerly and seemed confident of the response.

"I certainly do not consider it necessary in order that a man should abstain from the use of liquor, that he should write his name on a bit of paper."

"But hasn't it been repeatedly proved that the pledge has been a help to people?" Dell asked earnestly. "Haven't we numerous instances on record? Haven't there been those who signed the pledge, and in a moment of great temptation broken it, and then have of their own accord signed it again, feeling conscious that it was a help to them?"

"There have been instances undoubtedly wherein men considered themselves helped by the pledge, and we are bound to believe them."

"Then why is it not right to promote its circulation, so long as it is agreed that it may be a help to some, and certainly it can do no injury?"

"All are not agreed on that point, you know." Mr.

Tresevant's reply was very kind and smiling. Truth to tell, Dell did not know it; at least she did not know that Christian people differed.

She spoke in a dismayed tone. "Do *you* think it does injury, Mr. Tresevant?"

"I think there are natures that it might injure. I should hesitate to press a pledge of that nature upon persons."

"Will you be kind enough to tell me why?"

"Well, I am not sure that I can do so briefly; there is much that might be said. But you are aware, of course, that many persons, I might almost say most persons, are impelled strongly to do that which they have promised not to do. So that I have no doubt that oftentimes the pledge creates, or at least stimulates, the desire."

Dell surveyed him in unaffected amazement, and her voice had almost a touch of scorn, as she asked:

"Is it then only the total abstinence pledge that works in this manner; or do you really think that the command 'Thou shalt not steal' is the author of all the dishonesty that there is in the world?"

Mr. Tresevant laughed. "You are a causist, Miss Bronson, are you not?" he asked with unfailing courtesy.

"But," said Dell, "I don't understand. I am sure we do not consider other promises as having such disastrous results. Church pledges, bank pledges, marriage vows, the whole long list of promises, given and received daily, in the social and business world, nobody seems to have conscientious scruples against them."

"There is scarcely such a drawing away toward the breaking of any of these as there often is in the case of the total abstinence pledge."

"But is the boy who promises his mother never to touch wine, who when pressed by evil companions to drink answers nobly: 'I cannot; I promised Mother I wouldn't,' really weakened, injured by his promise?"

"Well," said Mr. Tresevant, smiling, "that is putting the case somewhat strongly perhaps. I would not be understood to be out of sympathy with the temperance reform. Intemperance is a gigantic evil, and it is right to combat it; only of course people must be allowed to choose their own weapons, and to think less of some than of others."

"What weapon would you recommend in the place of the temperance pledge?" Dell asked the question dryly.

"The great weapon to be used above all others, against the sin and suffering that can be found in this world, is the religion of Jesus Christ," answered Mr. Tresevant solemnly, looking and speaking as though he considered himself as having made an unanswerable remark. But the answer, or rather the next question, was quick and pointed.

"Then you consider that a man who has been persuaded to sign a total abstinence pledge is a less hopeful subject of divine grace than a drunkard is?"

What answer the minister of the gospel would have made to this very singular and troublesome question cannot be known; Mr. Elliot came to the rescue.

"But surely total abstinence and temperance are two different subjects. Aren't you confounding them, Miss Bronson?"

"I hardly call them distinct subjects, Mr. Elliot, and, therefore, of course, cannot confound them."

Mr. Elliot looked annoyed. "But you certainly do not think that every man who occasionally drinks a glass of wine or even of cider is going to become a drunkard? I see your pledge even prohibits cider."

"I think that I do not know anything about it, and cannot possibly tell unless I meet him twenty years from now, or more likely in a much shorter period of time; but this I do certainly know, that every poor drunkard on earth today began by drinking an occasional glass of wine or cider. I believe it is well known that men do not plunge into drunkenness as they do into the river to commit suicide; and I do sincerely believe the Christian standpoint to be 'Look not upon it!' The law of expediency ought to prove that, even to those who have no fears for themselves."

"But, Miss Bronson, you involve yourself in logical difficulties, do you not, when you take such ground?" It was the soft, calm voice of the minister who spoke now. "For instance, there are people in this world who just as certainly kill themselves from overeating, as others do from overdrinking. Should you then, as a Christian woman, abstain from the use of food?"

"Yes," said Dell coldly. "Just as soon as I discover that a large proportion of my brothers and sisters are ruining their bodies and wrecking their souls, not only for time but for eternity, and bringing absolute and hopeless ruin on their families from overeating; and as soon as I discover that I am setting them an example, when food is not only not a necessity of life at all, nor even conducive to health, but is on the contrary considered by eminent men a positive injury, just so soon will I consider it my duty to abstain from the use of food."

At this point, with a good deal of bang and scuffle, Mr. Bronson appeared on the scene. Mr. Tresevant immediately arose and courteously extended his hand, Mr. Elliot followed his example, and Dell brought forward a chair, which she had no sooner done than she was sorry for it. Her father's unusually talkative mood proved to her that he had been taking much more than his usual amount of liquor. And when he abruptly called her to account for not treating her friends, and opening the hall door screamed loudly to Sam to "bring the best brandy there was in the bar," her misery was at its height. He talked on loud and fast, until Sam having promptly obeyed his order, the host took the salver from his hand and approached the clergyman.

"What! You won't drink?" he said, in apparent surprise, as Mr. Tresevant refused. "Oh, well, you're a parson; we must excuse you, I suppose, though I've heard say you was a good hand at cider, and I'll be hanged if I haven't seen a man get drunker than a fool on cider. Well, my heart, you and I will have a drink together, anyhow; we ain't parsons."

Mr. Elliot, being divided between his desire not to anger the drunken man and not to utterly offend Dell, stood irresolute. Not so Dell. She came around to her father's side, laid her hand on his shoulder, and spoke in low, firm tones:

"Father, I consider that any guest of mine who drinks a drop of liquor in my presence has insulted me."

"That being the case," said Mr. Elliot, quickly and soothingly, "I am sure Mr. Bronson will excuse me." Then immediately both gentlemen arose to depart, as Mr. Bronson, staring and muttering ominously, finally backed out of the room with his refreshments. Dell, standing before them, ghastly pale even to her lips, said, still speaking in low, cold tones:

"I am sure, after this scene, the gentlemen will be prepared to excuse my extreme total abstinence principles. There was a time, not many years ago, when my father only took an occasional glass of cider."

11

HOW TO TEACH RECKLESS BOYS

I came not to call the righteous, but sinners to repentance.

THEY are a very wild set," said Mr. Nelson; "in fact, I am not sure that there are five wilder young men in the factory."

"That is encouraging!" Dell said.

"Well, in one sense it is, perhaps; at least it is very astonishing that they are willing to come to Sunday school even once more."

"Have they been before?"

"Oh, yes, several times; never for two Sabbaths in succession. We don't expect that. We have had very queer times with them; once they left in the midst of the exercises, and once they got into such uproarious laughter that the teacher left them in a huff or a fright, I hardly know which. It was unfortunate anyway, for since that time their aim has been to dispose of every teacher given them. I think that is their principal object in being willing to try Sunday school again."

"And you want me to try to teach such a class?" Dell exclaimed in amazement.

"That is precisely what I want," he answered, laughing. "You see, Miss Bronson, it resolves itself into this," speaking seriously now, and earnestly; "there is absolutely no one else, not a single person, who is willing to make the attempt. I have asked Mr. Tresevant, but he assures me he cannot. I think he is not disposed to risk the chances; they would be more than likely to make sport of every thing he said, and I fancy he does not like to compromise his dignity. Perhaps he is right; besides, he has a very important class of good Christian young ladies. Miss Emmeline Elliot is one of them; it is next to impossible to beg a teacher from his class, for a temporary supply, they are so much attached to their teacher."

"Mr. Nelson," said Dell, who had been thinking her own thoughts during the time, "what do you honestly suppose I could do with such a class as you describe?"

"That I honestly don't know," he answered, laughing again. "I am extremely anxious to try you, and so discover; or, more truthfully, I really don't expect you to do much of anything with them. I don't think anyone can; but what I want to avoid is the necessity of saying to them, 'Boys, you may come to the Sunday school of course, but we haven't a man or woman in our church who dares to undertake the charge of you as a class; therefore you must be teacherless.' That is about what they expect, and they delight in the thought. Now I did not come to you having any hope that you would grant my request; it is a strange one to make to a young lady; but as I told you before, you are my last resort; and if these fellows are willing to come inside the church, if only for one Sabbath, isn't it a pity to lose the chance of saying something that might possibly do them good?"

Dell made apparently an irrelevant response:

"Mr. Nelson, you are really the strangest man I ever met in my life."

Mr. Nelson, turned thus suddenly from the subject that engrossed his thoughts, elevated his eyebrows and looked astonished.

"I am! That amazes me. I thought I was very commonplace. May I inquire your meaning?"

"Why, your conversation would lead me constantly to suppose that your life was permeated with a high Christian principle; and yet you disclaim all title to the name Christian. I do not understand it."

"I think I may say that I am actuated by principle," he said, smiling gravely. "The principle of love to the whole human race."

"Then I cannot see how you can help owning allegiance to Him, who so loved the whole human race that he not only died for them, but lived for them solely, on this weary earth, for long, long years!" Dell spoke quickly, and with tones full of deep feeling. Her companion was entirely grave now, and apparently sad. After a little silence, he said, slowly and earnestly, "'By their fruits ye shall know them.' That is a Bible doctrine, is it not? I shall have to confess to you that the fruits which have fallen under my knowledge have not been such as to lead me to admire the tree on which they grew."

"Have you no exceptions to make?"

He answered her quickly, "Oh, yes, indeed, I would not have you think me so cynical. Yes, I have known noble Christian men and women and admired them; but, pardon me, they really seemed to be the exceptions."

There stood on the table beside Dell a neglected dish of fruit; all the good apples had been culled, leaving only the gnarled, knurly ones. She seized upon one that chanced to be very small, very worm-eaten, and beginning to decay, and, holding it up by the stem, said quickly, "Ought you to judge of the fruit of the apple tree by this specimen?"

He looked steadily and gravely at the apple, then at her, then smiling he bowed slightly and said, "I accept your rebuke. But, Miss Bronson, what about my boys? Are they doomed to go teacherless?"

"Why don't you take them yourself, Mr. Nelson?"

"There are two reasons: In the first place, I have a class that I gathered at infinite pains; they have never had another teacher, and no other stands ready to take them; and secondly, now I shall run the risk of appearing inconsistent again, but I do feel the need of securing for them a teacher who knows experimentally about this high Christian principle of which you speak."

Dell was silent and thoughtful; there was an old sentence sounding through her brain: "Whatsoever thy hand findeth to do," and yet another: "Whatsoever he saith unto you, do it." Who was she that she had a right to hesitate? "What do you mean by their being a wild set?" she asked suddenly. "How wild are they?"

"Oh, they swear outrageously, and smoke profusely, and gamble whenever they get a chance, not often for money, for they have very little of that article about them; but for raisins, or pins, or straws, or anything that is convenient, and they use liquor freely, every one of them."

"Mr. Nelson," said Dell earnestly, "I'm afraid I should miserably fail with such a class, and wouldn't that be worse for them than if I had not tried?"

"They have had no other teaching than continued failures; they never had the same teacher twice, as no one would attempt it a second time; and we have managed to be very unfortunate in our selections; one began at once to talk to them personally about their wicked ways; another addressed them solemnly as my dear young friends; and one tried to give them the story of Samuel. So you see you start with at least equal hopes of success; besides, what do you Christian people believe in regard to these matters? Have I not heard something about not leaning on an arm of flesh?"

A little silence fell between them, but at last Dell broke it.

"Well, Mr. Nelson, I will do the very best I can."

Thus it came to pass that Dell Bronson, daintily clothed in purest white, stood in the doorway of the old church on the next Sabbath morning, waiting for Mr. Nelson to show her to her class.

"Are they here?" she asked as he came toward her.

"Every one of them excessively amused over their own wit, and ready for almost anything. So am I. I declare to you I shall not be surprised in the least to be called on to help quell a riot. I don't know what turn their fun will take."

"I don't know whether I can do ànything with them or not, but I am going to try," Dell answered, with that peculiar note in her voice that always gave one courage.

"Mr. Nelson, I want their names on a card; do they know that I am to be their teacher?"

Mr. Nelson shook his head. "I speculated some little time as to whether I would inform them. I finally decided not. I didn't like to risk it. Here are the names. Shall I go in and give you a formal introduction?"

Dell took the card and studied it carefully. "Jack Cooley, Jim Forbes, John Barney, Dick Holmes, Henry Day."

"Do you suppose I shall ever know more about them personally than I do today?"

Mr. Nelson shook his head. "I will neither encourage nor discourage you. I am in as noncommittal a state of mind as can be imagined."

"That is remarkable encouragement," Dell said, smiling. "No, thank you, I mean to introduce myself."

Then she went in and took a seat in front of the five boys. They looked at her and at each other, chuckled and whistled not very loud, and made observations about her in a not very undertone. She turned toward them the moment the opening exercises were concluded, with a very cheery "Good morning, young gentlemen. I don't know but you have the advantage of me. I presume you know that I am Miss Bronson, while I know your names, it is true, but haven't an idea which name belongs to which person. I shall have to ask your help. Will you be kind enough to tell me which is Mr. Cooley?"

If Dell had only known it, she had taken them at a disadvantage; they had been taught, or at least talked at, by middle-aged gentlemen in spectacles, by middle-aged ladies with severely rebuking faces, people who had evinced more or less embarrassment or bewilderment, as if they had said, "How *shall* we approach these young savages!" But they had never in their lives before come in contact with a young, pretty, exquisitely dressed lady, who surveyed them with utmost composure, without a trace of bewilderment or embarrassment, who addressed them with courteous politeness, as became a young lady speaking to young gentlemen. Not a single one of them laughed as they had previously expected to do; and the corner one answered promptly, "My name's Cooley."

"Well, then, Mr. Cooley," Dell said, holding out her

hand, with a bright smile, "will you introduce me to the rest of the friends?"

Which Mr. Cooley, much to his own amazement, found himself doing, in a fashion somewhat unlike ordinary introduction to be sure, but it answered Dell's purpose very well. After a few minutes of preliminary talk she suddenly asked a question which seemed to greatly astonish them, yet it was simply:

"Are you interested in the lesson for today?"

Now it had never before seemed to occur to any of these teachers that there was a possibility of their being interested in any lesson whatever; so they stared at each other and laughed a little; finally Mr. Cooley ventured to remark:

"We ain't no kind of an idea where the lesson is."

"Oh, you have not studied it then?" the innocent teacher said, speaking as if that were a matter of surprise. "Then of course you will not be particularly interested in it. I find it is a lesson that requires a great deal of study. I have spent about four hours on it this week."

At which remark Jim Forbes was very much amazed. "For the land's sake!" he said earnestly. "How many verses is there in it?"

And upon being informed that there were only seven, he said with a contemptuous air that he would bet a goose that he could learn them seven verses in a good deal less than four hours.

"Oh, it wasn't the committing to memory that took so long," Dell explained, "but there was so much to think about in it all. It is about the blind man, you know, who sat by the wayside begging. He called to Jesus, you remember, as soon as he heard that he was passing by, and begged for his sight to be restored, and Jesus heard his call and gave him his sight; and I spent a good deal of time in trying to find out why the story was put in the Bible for us to read, and how many points of similarity there were between this blind man and the people around us nowadays who are blind, and the more I thought about it all, the more interested I became."

"Did you find out what they put it in the Bible for?" Dick Holmes questioned.

"Why, yes," said Dell. "I think I found some reasons. It is apt to give us confidence in a physician, you know, when we hear of wonderful cures that he has performed; then the thought that interested me greatly was that the blind man seemed entirely conscious of his own state; he appeared to be fully convinced that he was blind."

"I don't think that's anything great," Jim Forbes said contemptuously. "I should think a fellow might find out mighty quick whether he was blind or not."

"I don't know. I was thinking he might have argued something like this: 'I don't believe I'm blind; people make a great fuss about seeing. I don't think it amounts to much. I shouldn't wonder if I can see as well as anybody can. What is seeing, anyway? Very likely there is no such thing!' Haven't you heard people argue something in that way about things of which they know nothing?"

Jack Cooley laughed; he had, he said, but Dick Holmes was ready for an argument.

"Yes, but you can prove to a blind man that he can't see, because you can describe things to him that he knows he never saw."

"But how are you going to make him believe that you have ever seen them? Can't I, being a Christian, describe things to a person that he knows he has never felt, and won't he be very likely to say, 'That's all imagination on her part; I don't believe a word of it'?"

Then several of the others laughed and looked curiously at Dick, because this was precisely what he was in the habit of saying. Their looks made him reckless, and he spoke with an air of defiance:

"Well, I don't. I don't believe anything. I think these Bible stories are all humbug. I don't believe there ever was any blind man that got his sight again in the way it tells about. I think religion is all a pack of lies!"

Then he folded his arms and sat back triumphantly and waited for the shocked look that he delighted to bring to people's faces; but he looked in vain; Dell's face was as serene as a summer morning.

"Yes," she said placidly, as if she might perhaps agree with every word he said. "But, Mr. Holmes, you said you didn't believe *anything.* Of course you didn't quite mean that. Don't you believe, for instance, that people die?"

Mr. Holmes started, but admitted that he did.

"You really have no doubt about it, have you, but that all the people in this world will die?"

No; he hadn't the least doubt about that.

"Well, now, my Bible states that fact distinctly, stated it hundreds of years ago, not only that everybody would die, but what would be about the average length of life; and I find that it has made no mistake; there has been not even one exception to the law. I find that you believe so much unhesitatingly. Now just suppose, for argument's sake, that everything else that the Bible states should happen to be true as this is? There are certain things that in one sense we cannot prove until we die, but since we know that we have got to die, wouldn't it be wise to be on the safe side;

have the chances of securing all the joy that the Bible tells of, if there *should* be any such thing to secure?"

It was a strange way of putting the question. A new way to them; they looked at each other in puzzled silence; that the thought interested them was certain, and Dell had very little difficulty in keeping up the interest to the end. It was a rather strangely conducted lesson; not at all in the orthodox style, Dell was certain; but the superintendent's bell rang while they were still sitting thoughtful and quiet, boldly discussing questions that no one had ever permitted them to broach before.

"Did you give them a morphine powder?" Mr. Nelson questioned, with a look of puzzled wonder, as he met Dell in the hall. "I certainly never knew them to be quiet before."

And Dell's answer was:

"Mr. Nelson, they every one promised me that they would come next Sabbath."

12

THE TEMPERANCE DIALOGUE

Vow, and pay unto the Lord your God.

DELL had been very busy for two weeks. Mr. Nelson's last brilliant idea had occupied all her leisure time. It was complete now in all its details, the girls were perfect in their parts, and the eventful evening had arrived. They were to have another temperance meeting, the distinguished feature of which was to be an original colloquy, subject—The Pledge, performed by members of the Society.

It had not been announced who the author was, and only Dell and Mr. Nelson knew. To show you in what degree the new idea succeeded, I will give you the performance entire. First in order was the reading of the pledge by Mr. Nelson. And the pledge was worded thus:

"I hereby solemnly promise to abstain from the use or sale of all spirituous or malt liquors, wine, or cider, as a beverage."

Then Tommy Truman had a word to say.

"Is there a father or mother who loves his or her children who would not be glad to have the names of those children on this pledge? Is there a sister, a child, a wife, a Sunday school teacher, who would not rejoice over the added names of their dear ones? Can there be any good reason for refusing to sign the pledge? Can there be two sides to this question? Are we not all agreed?"

His sturdy little friend and fellow-signer, Harry Mason, made the somewhat pompous answer: "There *are* undoubtedly two sides to this question; many persons differ, and may we not say differ *honestly,* from the views that have been expressed? At any rate, they would like to be heard before being condemned. Are there not thousands of people, good people too, who never touch the accursed thing, and yet sign no pledge?"

Tommy Truman responded: "Is that an argument, my friend? I can't see how your thousands would be worse off if they proclaimed their temperance principles by signing the pledge, and thus helped others to know where they stood."

Harry answered with indignant eyes and puffy cheeks: "But can't you trust a man when he promises you, without putting that promise on paper?"

"Why, yes," said Tommy, "of course you can. Don't you ever take a man's note when he owes you money; nor ask for a receipt when you pay him a thousand dollars? You must trust him, you know, without his name on a paper. How would your argument work (if you call it an argument) on any question but temperance?"

Tom Stuart was on hand next. "Our friend forgets too that we don't ask his name on the pledge because we do not trust him without it, but to help him to trust himself. Every honest man knows that his determination to do or not to do a thing grows stronger and firmer every time he commits himself in words or on paper; every true man honors his promise, and, if he means it, he is not ashamed to confirm his own resolution by putting his name to it."

Then Harry, contemptuously: "Let the weak ones sign it then; we who are strong and have principle need not pledge."

It was Mr. Nelson's kind, grave voice that made answer: "We then that are strong are to bear the infirmities of the weak, and not to please ourselves."

There was a Mary Truman, who now took up the question: "But suppose we sign the pledge and break it. Would not that be a great sin? Is it not better to drink wine a hundred times than to break one promise? Think of the multitudes who have done this. Besides being drunkards, they are covenant breakers. So if I sign the pledge and break it, what then?"

Tommy's answer burst forth: "I say shame on you. And again I say, sign to keep and not to break. 'No drunkard shall inherit the kingdom of heaven,' my Bible says. Do you suppose it will be a comfort for a lost soul, when he lifts his eyes, being in torment, to remember that he never signed the pledge? If you are afraid you will break the pledge, then you are in danger already, and who more than you needs the restraining power of a sacred pledge? Afraid you may break it and go back? Why, you are back now. You are the very one who needs help, and if you have any regard for your word, the pledge will help you."

Will Jones was the next speaker: "I have no desire to make a display of my temperance principles. How many people sign the pledge because they would have people think them very good and self-denying? I have seen enough of this empty pretense, this temperance hypocrisy, whereby people drink on the sly, and yet get a name for abstinence. 'Let not your left hand know what your right hand doeth.'"

Susy Carter answered him: "That's the queerest argument I have ever heard yet, and I have heard some queer ones. I won't write any letters to my friends, for that would be making a parade of my affections. There are people in this world who cheat; therefore, I won't profess not to. People sign the pledge and drink 'on the sly'; that was the refined expression that was used, I believe; therefore, I won't sign it unless I may drink 'on the *sly*' too. Is that it? Then the idea of quoting from the Bible to match that style of argument! It must be the only verse that gentleman knows; he cannot, at least, have come across the one that declares, 'By their fruits you shall know them'; or, 'Neither do men light a candle and put it under a bushel, but on a candlestick, and it giveth light unto all that are in the house'; or this: 'Let your light so shine before men, that they may see your good works and glorify your Father which is in heaven.'"

There was a nice, oldish lady, deeply interested in the temperance cause, who had been coaxed into service, and who now popped up and spoke earnestly: "For my part, I don't see no great difference between drinking brandy, and wine, and cider and eating it; and so long as you folks like mince pies, and nice sauce, and things, as well as you do, you hadn't ought to come down on them that makes them for you."

Her own grandson, a splendid young fellow, answered her: "I agree with you in that matter. It is as well to drink as to eat brandy. But, Grandma, can't you make mince pies without brandy? And is there no other delicious sauce but this? Are we indeed as badly off about our food as was Miss Flora McFlimsey about her finery? She had forty dresses, yet nothing to wear. Our heavenly Father has filled the world full of good things, and yet without mince pies, mixed with brandy, we are in danger of starvation!"

Miss Lilly Archer asked the next question: "May I ask abstainers if any such pledge as the one given here this evening can be found in our Bible? The very last chapter warns against adding anything to this sacred book. Will not those abstainers be cursed for being wise above what is written? Before I sign this pledge, I must have a 'Thus saith the Lord.'"

Tommy Truman was ready with an answer: "But they said, 'We will drink no wine: for Jonadab, the son of Rechab, our father, commanded us, saying, Ye shall drink no wine, neither ye nor your sons forever. Thus have we obeyed the voice of Jonadab, the son of Rechab, our father, in all that he hath charged us, to drink no wine all our days, we, our wives, our sons, nor our daughters.' That's Bible! Doesn't it sound somewhat like a pledge? Perhaps you would like also to hear something about the Nazarites' temperance pledge, and Daniel's, and Jeremiah's, and Paul's. The Bible is verily good enough temperance pledge for me."

Then Fred Edson had a word to say: "But did not Noah drink freely, and wasn't he a good man? Did not the priests and kings of Judah? Did not Jesus? They called him a wine bibber. And were not the disciples in the habit of drinking all they wished? Peter, in his great Pentecostal sermon, does not deny that his friends were very fond of wine; he merely says they were not drunk so early in the morning. At the Communion table, did not the Savior command them to drink the wine? 'Drink ye all of it.' Then remember what Paul tells young Timothy: 'Take a little wine for thy stomach's sake.' What can you say to that?"

Tommy Truman was ready for him: "I can say—are

you Timothy? Have you Timothy's complaint? Has Paul examined your physical disorder and directed wine; and have you some of Timothy's wine? 'Noah drank freely,' you say. Yes, and got drunk; therefore we must. Solomon had many wives; must we? David committed murder. Peter took the name of God in vain. You say, Christ commanded them to drink wine, and you might have added that he changed water into wine; therefore, it is wicked to pledge against wine; we *must* drink. But what if that wine which Jesus made at the marriage in Cana, and that made at the communion, and that recommended by Paul to Timothy, was all new, the fresh juice of the grape? Then where is your Bible for touching the filthy, poisoning stuff sold in barrooms and saloons, a compound of Prussic acid, cocculus indicus, alum, Brazil wood, gypsum, lead, copperas, sulphuric acid, logwood, muriatic acid, lavender, cloves, and rosemary?"

Then young Williams: "Oh, do stop this talk about poison. Doesn't the Bible say, 'Every creature of God is good, and nothing to be refused?' Isn't wine a good creature of God? Has the Creator taken so much pains to make all these things, and shall we call them nasty poisons? Let us beware how we pour contempt on the word of God, and on his good creatures."

This brought Edward Phillips to his feet with glowing face: "Every creature of God is good. Good to eat and drink you mean? Rattlesnakes are creatures, so are crows; would you like a dish of them to eat? How about poison ivy, quicksilver, and nitric acid? God takes pains to make all these creatures; therefore, if we do not drink them, let us beware how we pour contempt upon the Bible! Is that the argument?"

Fred Edson, meantime, seemed to have thought of a new idea: "But are we not called unto liberty, while this pledge of yours makes one a slave; it binds one hand and foot, puts a lock on one's mouth, when he is ready to die with thirst? Did not our forefathers bleed and die to eat and drink what they could? Have you never seen the Declaration of Independence and its list of glorious signers? You have surely heard how when Washington put his name there, he said, 'Give me liberty or give me death!' Shall I sign away my liberty? Never!"

Edward Phillips had not yet exhausted his fund of sarcasm: "Liberty!" he repeated in scornful tones. "Liberty to drink rum! Liberty to reel through the streets! Liberty to fight and swear and roll in the gutter, to have a black eye and a bloated face, to have rags, poverty, and contempt. Liberty to bruise one's wife and beggar one's children! to end up in the prison or on the gallows! Is *this* liberty that our fathers bled and died for? Is this what our blessed Bible means when it says we are called unto liberty? Why, the pledge is the breaking of the prisoner's chains. It is the sign of liberty to be a sober, industrious Christian man."

Charlie Brown was the next speaker: "But this pledge makes cruel distinctions in society. *You* may be prepared to put yourself in a straitjacket; *you* may have no taste for intoxicating liquors. Water may satisfy you. Many others are not prepared for this sacrifice. Is it kind, is it polite, to ask others to sign a pledge that would be so hard for them to keep? Think how awkward such are made to feel, when your pledge is presented to them and they cannot sign it! Is it like a true wife to put down her name, and so place a bar between herself and her husband? Does not this interfere with the happiness of a husband and wife?"

"Humph!" said Tommy Truman. "That is, it would

make my neighbor feel uncomfortable if I should paint my house; therefore I must let it remain as rusty as his. If a lady's husband swears, so must she; if he chews tobacco, so must she; if he would sooner go to a horse race than a prayer meeting, must she go too? It might interfere with their mutual happiness if she should pledge herself to Christ. What must she do?"

Harry Mason interrupted him: "But cider is good. It is splendid when sucked through a straw. It is nice when friends come to spend an evening with you. It is very refreshing when you are tired, or cold, or thirsty, or hot, or when you have lost your appetite. Cider keeps me from the pledge, wine others, beer others. I do love cider. I make no concealments. Let us be frank. But I never expect to drink to excess, nor to drink hard cider."

"Cider is good, you say," said Tom Stuart. "How much does that remark mean? If you are talking about nutriment, there is more nutriment in one pound of beefsteak than in a whole barrel of cider. Apple juice ferments in twenty-four hours after being pressed from the fruit, yet you are not going to drink hard cider! Hard cider contains more alcohol than lager beer, porter, or ale. At a meeting where there were sixty reformed drunkards, the question was asked, 'How many of you believe that you could not drink one glass of the mildest liquor without going back to your former habits?' Every one of the sixty arose to their feet; they evidently considered cider a dangerous drink. A few years since, a young man in Massachusetts learned to like cider by sucking it through a straw; at fourteen his daily beverage was cider, and he would become beastly drunk; at eighteen his father offered him a farm if he would sign the pledge. His answer was, 'I'd rather have my cider.' At twenty-three he was in a drunkard's grave! Yet my friend here says, 'Cider is good.'"

By this time Mary Truman had found voice again: "But what, pray, will become of the great army of brewers and distillers, saloon keepers, bartenders, and others, if we all sign the pledge and don't patronize them anymore. Going to let them starve?"

Her brother answered her briefly and sharply: "Let them go to work like honest men."

Lilly Archer curled her pretty nose as she said: "So many of your pledgers are such outrageous fanatics."

"Better be a fanatic than a drunkard," said Tom Stuart shortly.

There was a bright-eyed little girl sitting near Mr. Nelson; he suddenly turned toward her and said pleasantly, "Laura, I have a request to make of you."

"A request!" she repeated, with wondering eyes.

"Yes. Do you know I want you to sign this pledge?"

"Why, what possible good would that do? I am not in danger."

"Every one is in danger, my child."

"Men and boys, you mean, Mr. Nelson."

"I mean women as well as men, girls as well as boys. You, young as you are, are not *too* young, or too wise, or too strong to escape. He 'goeth about as a roaring lion, seeking whom he may devour.' Besides, you have influence. Laura, if *you* sign, you may save someone; if you refuse, you may ruin someone."

"If I really thought I had any influence, or could be the means of helping anyone, I would sign it. I think I will do it, Mr. Nelson."

"Thank you," Mr. Nelson said, with a bright smile. "More than this audience are rejoicing over your decision. Truman, will you pass the pledge book this way?"

The young girl's cheeks flushed a deeper red, and she said in some confusion:

"Do you really mean I am to sign it now?"

"Now, why not? 'Do with thy might what thy hand findeth to do.'"

"But before all the people. Isn't there time enough, Mr. Nelson?"

"'Let your light so shine before men,'" quoted Mr. Nelson, meaningly; and without more ado Laura wrote her name.

"Now, Laura, I wish I could get you and all young ladies to make one more promise. That you would never marry a man who refuses to sign the pledge."

This was evidently putting the matter a little too strongly for Tom Stuart: "But Mr. Nelson," he said, "what if a man entirely worthy of Miss Laura in every other respect, and truly loving her, refuses to sign the pledge; should she have nothing to do with him?"

"I do not believe, Tom, that a man who will not shut, and lock, and bolt, and bar the door between himself and strong drink ever does truly love, honor, and respect a woman. That is taking strong ground, you think, but I have lived more years and watched this matter longer than you have. I tell you it is dangerous."

Laura had been listening, her large eyes fixed intently on the speaker, and suddenly she said, "I promise. I do promise."

Mr. Nelson answered quickly, "Thank God. May you be helped to keep your vows."

13

A Strange Scene in a Barroom

I will never leave thee nor forsake thee.

DELL and Mr. Tresevant walked homeward, a fair share of the way, in almost absolute silence. Dell ventured a remark or two about the beauty of the evening, but she received absentminded replies, until she began to wonder why he did not go his own homeward way and commune with his own thoughts without disturbance, if such were his desire. At last she broke the silence and spoke in mischievous tone:

"Mr. Tresevant, why don't you criticize our performance this evening?"

"How do you know I am in a critical mood?" he asked quietly.

"Oh, I know you are longing to disapprove of a dozen things that were said and done; I can see it in your face; the moonlight is very bright, you know. Besides, I looked at you twice during the evening."

He laughed a little at that, then said gravely, "Since you read my face so well, I may as well confess to you that I did entirely disapprove of the tenor of the arguments tonight. I do not know whom I am censuring, probably Mr. Nelson; he is not a Christian man, and, therefore, we must not expect much of him, but I can but wish that he were more careful of his choice of language."

"If you mean the exercise," Dell answered promptly, "it was not his language at all; the exercise was selected."

"Well, in his selections then. I think it was a most unfortunate thing." Mr. Tresevant was growing excited; he spoke very earnestly, a little hotly Dell thought. She felt perfectly composed and good-humored. She had not expected Mr. Tresevant to be pleased, knowing perfectly well that the arguments trenched too closely on his views to be agreeable.

"Will you enlighten us as to the unfortunateness of our evening's work?" she said, still speaking gaily. "Because we are pluming ourselves on the fact that it passed off delightfully, and perhaps it is as well to have our pride somewhat subdued."

"I know you are not in sympathy with my views, Miss Bronson. I know you feel deeply on this subject. I honor you for it; if you carry the feeling to almost an extreme, it is not in the least to be wondered at. But aside from your personal feeling, let me ask you, do you think it right to hold the pastor of a church up to ridicule before his own young people, be the subject what it may? May he not honestly differ in opinion with one member of his congregation without thus being made the subject of public sarcasm?"

Now, indeed, Dell was dismayed. She spoke hurriedly and eagerly: "Mr. Tresevant, I do earnestly assure you that nothing of the sort was intended or implied. I am posted in this matter, and the principal actors in it would be utterly shocked and grieved did they suppose that you for a moment imagined such a thing."

Mr. Tresevant smiled loftily. "I do not doubt your

sincerity," he said kindly. "It is evident that you do not share the feeling which I am certain exists; but allow me to remind you that I am older than you, and have probably seen more of the wrong side of the world. You are kind enough to believe that the exercise of the evening was selected. I believe nothing of the sort. I consider Mr. Nelson entirely capable of having written it, and I have not the least doubt but that he did so, and it was most closely and unkindly aimed at me throughout. I confess I once thought him more of a gentleman than to be guilty of so small a thing, but I must change my mind."

Dell's voice lost its touch of dismayed distress; it was cold and had a touch of hauteur, as she said:

"You have an undoubted right to believe what you please, a right which you seem bent on gratifying to the utmost tonight; therefore I cannot know that you will please to believe me when I tell you that Mr. Nelson never heard one word of the exercise until this evening, and that it was prepared by my Uncle Edward and myself before I had so much as heard of your existence, so that I am at a loss to understand how it could be considered a personal attack, unless it touched you so nearly that you must accept it as belonging to you."

It was Mr. Tresevant's turn to be dismayed.

"Miss Bronson, I beg your pardon," he said in a voice full of distress. "I did not imagine——I assure you I had no idea——I do hope you will overlook my language."

"There is no occasion to apologize," Dell said gaily, her good humor having returned. "Indeed, you have quite honored me in appropriating my wisdom as Mr. Nelson's, and if I have proved to you that personality was the furthest from my thoughts, I think I have fairly earned the right to hear your criticisms."

"I am sorry that while I admire the genius displayed, I must be frank and not approve some of the arguments," he answered gravely.

"I am not sorry at all. I knew you would not approve. What I want to know now is the reason why?"

"Miss Bronson, haven't we been all over the ground before?"

"Not a bit," Dell said promptly. "The arguments are not old ones; we consider that we advanced some, at least, that are original; now for your objections."

"I do not approve of exacting indiscriminate promises, especially from the young, for any purpose whatever."

"Nor do I. But how does your remark apply to us? The promise asked for tonight applied to something very definite, very simple, and something that had been very carefully explained."

"Have you an idea that the promise extorted from that child tonight, in regard to her sometime in the future marrying somebody, will be in the least likely to be kept, provided it conflicts with her future wishes?"

"I don't know," Dell answered gravely. "But, Mr. Tresevant, the same child united with your church two weeks ago; have you an idea that she will keep the solemn promise that you—I will not say extorted from her, although I think there certainly was as much appearance of extortion as there was in our meeting this evening?"

"If she does keep it—," he answered her, in some heat and ignoring the question she asked, "if she *does* keep it, I think you have laid her under a cruel obligation; one that may be the cause of great and unnecessary suffering. The man who seeks her for a wife might be in every way worthy of her, and yet have conscientious scruples against signing a pledge. How can you think it right to fetter people thus?"

Then Dell did a most disrespectful thing. She laughed, but she immediately apologized for it.

"I beg pardon, Mr. Tresevant; you undoubtedly have a right to your own views, and I suppose I have a right to consider them absurd, if I choose; but if you wish me to define my opinion, it is simply that a good man, who has considered the magnitude of the evils of intemperance, and who has resolved in his heart and asked God to help him to do everything in his power by precept and example, and in every way that he thinks right to put down the evil, is in my estimation solemnly pledged; if he is conscientiously opposed to putting his name on a piece of paper, he is a mystery to be sure, and to me he would be an absurdity. I should consider him standing in his own light, and trampling on one means of usefulness, but that would not alter the nature of his solemn pledge between God and his own soul. But a man who was conscientiously opposed to pledges because he believed in temperance as opposed to total abstinence, because, in short, he liked wine, or beer, or cider, and meant to use it, I certainly would not marry; I would do anything in my power to keep a friend of mine from marrying him. Those are my solemn convictions of duty, Mr. Tresevant."

He answered her lightly, without a trace of his former interest:

"Miss Bronson, I propose that you and I raise a flag of truce. We shall probably never agree any better than we do now in our views on this subject, and we certainly can find pleasanter topics to discuss. I beg your pardon for having drawn you into this debate, I will endeavor not to transgress again." Then followed a few bright words from each in regard to other matters, and he left her at her father's door.

She went to her little back parlor and dropped herself wearily into a seat. That reaction which those who have felt understand so well, and dread so much, began to creep over her. She had worked hard and eagerly for this evening, she had assumed much care and responsibility, and what had been accomplished? Nothing, it seemed to her; she even doubted whether the exercise was not a failure; if only Uncle Edward had been there to help and comment. "If he were only here now," this poor, lonely girl said aloud, "or if I were there, sitting on the low seat by Aunt Laura, with her hand just touching my hair, and Uncle Edward going over the evening and pointing out what we could do to improve the next effort. Oh, Uncle and Auntie, I want you; I need you. Oh, pshaw!" This last as a sort of rallying cry to her drooping heart. "You must not desert me," she said to her weary spirits. "This is not Boston, and I am not Uncle Edward; if I were it would be a nicer world, but since I am only myself, we must do what we can and be cheerful over it." She gathered up her fallen hat and gloves and passed out into the hall. There was much loud talking in the barroom, among which she could distinguish her father's voice and her own name. "My Dell will beat all the singing you ever heard tell of," he was saying earnestly. "I declare now if you shan't have a specimen," and just as Dell was passing the door he swung it open and spoke to her.

"I declare, here you are! I'm in the very nick of time; I was coming to hunt you. Just you come in now and give us a song. Steve here has been bragging like all possessed about his girl's singing, and I tell him I know she can't begin to compare with mine, and I want you to come and prove it." Saying which he took hold of her arm and tried to draw her in. There was necessity for very rapid thinking on Dell's part. Her father had been drinking, not so much as he often did, but enough to render him incapable of seeing the impropriety of his direction; there were four others in the barroom, all of them in different stages of intoxication; one of them, a young man, seemed to have some faint gleams of sense left in his confused brain, for he muttered:

"Oh, now, Bronson, that's, that's rather mean taking advantage of a girl; let her go now, that's a good fellow!"

What should she do? Here was her father, talking eagerly and gently pushing her in; yet there was a wild gleam in his eye suggestive of anything but gentleness, and there were no means of determining what he might not do if his anger were aroused by refusal. Yet could she come into that awful room and sing for those four drunkards? Was there any hope that song of hers might reach their hearts, through brains so befogged with liquor? Would she not in a sense be casting pearls before swine if she attempted to reach them in any way, while in that condition? What would Uncle Edward tell her to do if he were there? Should she try to get away and run the risk of maddening her father, losing for the future the influence that she now possessed over him? Oh, what would the Master tell her to do? "In season and out of season." Did it mean even at such times as these? And Dell Bronson lifted up her heart in "brief, earnest cry for help," then allowed herself to be drawn into the room, pushed the door behind her, and taking her station near it, behind a large chair, looking meantime, in her white robes and white face, like a pale spirit descended among them from another world, she suddenly let her pure, rich voice float through the room; her father dropped silently into a chair near her and listened, as every word came to their ears as distinctly as though she had been reading it:

> *Say, sinner! hath a voice within*
> *Oft whispered to thy secret soul,*
> *Urged thee to leave the ways of sin,*
> *And yield thy heart to God's control?*
>
> *Sinner! it was a heavenly voice—*
> *It was the Spirit's gracious call;*
> *It bade thee make the better choice,*
> *And haste to seek in Christ thine all.*
>
> *Spurn not the call to life and light;*
> *Regard, in time, the warning kind;*
> *That call thou may'st not always slight,*
> *And yet the gate of mercy find.*
>
> *Sinner, perhaps this very day,*
> *Thy last accepted time may be;*
> *Oh! should'st thou grieve Him now away,*
> *Then hope may never beam on thee.*

Even Dell herself was conscious of the fact that she had never sung before, as she sang those words that night. They seemed to be wrung from her very soul, and her listeners sat as if they felt something of their power. Through to the end, with clear, full tones, then as silently and swiftly as if she had indeed been a spirit, she turned and vanished from the room. She ran upstairs through the hall to her own room, and locked and bolted the door; then she flung herself on her knees and buried her head in the pillow, giving way to a perfect passion of tears—the utter desolation and bitterness of her lot rolled heavily upon her. What a humiliation had come over her. What would her Boston friends have thought to have found her singing songs in a barroom to a company of drunkards? And one of them her father! Oh, the bitterness of that thought. She felt utterly crushed and hopeless; her life seemed to her not worth a struggle. What had she accomplished? What could she accomplish? Who was there to help her? Even the minister of the gospel turned with cold eyes away from the work; had no words for it but those of discouragement. It was an hour of great and bitter sorrow. The bowed form shook and trembled with the strength of her pain; the poor motherless, worse than fatherless girl felt utterly desolate and alone. Gradually the stormy grief subsided, and her tears came quietly, and after a little there came to the lonely girl a sweet remembrance of the fact that she was not alone; that there was really no such thing as lonely hours for her; had not her Father said, "I will never leave thee nor forsake thee"?

"I am a weak, foolish child," she said aloud. "I constantly forget my Father's house and the room prepared for me there. I even forget my Father's presence and promise, and complain that I am alone and desolate. Oh, Father, forgive my murmuring, and teach me how to endure patiently, remembering that 'Thy ways are not as our ways.'"

14

A Trip to Boston

His ways are not our ways.

IT was another August day, hot and dusty, and altogether uncomfortable for most people. Dell did not
look uncomfortable. She stood framed in the doorway
of the old depot, exactly where she stood the first time
you ever heard of her. And but for the fact that the
linen suit was fresh and crisp, and the lawn ruffles at
neck and wrist perfectly pure and untravel-stained,
you might imagine that we had gone backward in our
story, and had just helped her off the cars, to make her
entree in Lewiston; so exactly in every other respect
did she look like that bright, young girl of whom we
told you. Yet she was really a year older, and had not
just alighted from the train, but was standing there
watching the man while he fastened the bit of brass
to her neat little trunk that was to see it safe to Boston.
It was just a year to a day since she had stood there
before and waited for her father. She thought of it, and
it sent her mind wandering back over the year. How
much she had meant to accomplish! A year had
seemed to her a long time, and she had almost expected to work miracles. She both smiled and sighed
as she thought of it that afternoon. Well, what had

123

been accomplished? There were times in which Dell's heart answered drearily, "Nothing, nothing!" The horrible old tavern still stood, and the dreadful bar still poured forth its poisons. Her father still drank his glasses of brandy, more glasses than he used to drink a year ago. Sam Miller still reeled home from time to time in the darkening twilight and whipped little Mamie and turned his wife out-of-doors. The loafers still spit and chewed in the barroom, just as many of them as heretofore. Mr. Tresevant still preached his sermons of a Sabbath in the horrible den of a church, still looked with grave, doubtful eyes on the temperance movement, and still remained conscientiously opposed to pledges. Young Mr. Elliot still drank his wine, in a gentlemanly way, when he was where respectable people could see him, and in a much more doubtful way sometimes, if report spoke truth; and a looker-on would have said that all things remained as they were before.

No, not all—the long, dirty piazza, where the spitting, chewing loafers sat that day and stared at Dell, was now in a new coat of paint, was spotlessly clean and neat, and absolutely bereft of loafers; there were things that Dell *would not* endure, and this, though apparently a trifle, was one of them. It was an innovation; the great leather-bottomed, high-backed armchairs had stood on that piazza as long and much longer than Dell could remember, and the chewing, and spitting, and chuckling had gone on from time immemorial. But when Dell had said, "They must do all such disgraceful work up inside, Father; I cannot have it on my nice, clean piazza," and saying it, had dropped her brown head a little on one side and spoken with a determined little ring to her voice, her father had remembered certain other innovations, such as clean rooms and exquisitely comfortable meals and no more fighting in the kitchen, and had chuckled a little, and admired his daughter immensely, and declared it should be as she said. So the piazza was purified, and the young men who boarded in the house came up clean steps, without the smell or touch of tobacco or whiskey. A little thing, very, but who is ever going to know but that it saved those young men? There were other little things: Sally and Kate in the kitchen, being still good Catholics, stood ready to fall down and worship their mistress, and in every way in their power aided and abetted her efforts; for hadn't Sally a lover, and didn't he now and then have a spree, and wasn't Miss Dell "ahelpin' him to overcome himself"? Then the temperance meeting, weak and small though it was, still lived, and there were two or three who had joined them that they did not expect; among others, the post office clerk who boarded at the hotel, and who used to take an occasional glass of wine. Then, and Dell's eyes brightened as she thought of that, her class—those five wild young men, her class still. Reformed, you probably think, become patterns to the rising youth of America. Very little of that, but—they came to Sunday school—came every Sunday, and were attentive and respectful to her, though hardly so to anyone else; and Dell was praying for them all, now hopefully, now despairingly, always persistently.

Mr. Tresevant came briskly down the straggling street, sprang up the steps, and held out his hand to Dell. "You meant to be in time, did you not, Miss Dell? I called to walk with you to the cars, but found you vanished."

Dell laughed. "I was in haste," she said naively. "And it seemed to me I should get on faster if I took an early start, but I don't see that I have made great speed thus far. Isn't the train late, Mr. Tresevant?"

"Not yet, certainly, as it is not due for ten minutes. What haste you are in to leave Lewiston. Has it then no attraction whatever for you? Are you always going to feel that there is no place in the world but Boston?" He spoke half reproachfully, but Dell had no answer for him; both eyes and thoughts were engaged elsewhere. One of her enemies in the shape of a cellar grocery, or, in other words, cellar rum shop, was directly across the street, and toward that fascinating spot shambled one whom she knew; she watched him eagerly until he neared the door, and then the only reply Mr. Tresevant received was an eager, "Isn't that Jim Forbes, Mr. Tresevant? Yes, I know it is." Then she called in clear, quick tones, "Mr. Forbes," and if a bombshell had exploded just ahead of him, the young man could not have turned more suddenly than he did at the sound of that voice. He came across the street, and Dell came down from the doorway and stood on the second step, smiling and cordial.

"Did you come up to see me off?" she asked, holding out her hand, which he grasped as if his had been an iron vise.

"No," he said, with an awkward laugh, "not exactly. I come to see myself off. I've got to go down to Boston to get an iron fixed."

"And you are going on this train? Why, then, I shall not have to travel alone after all. That's nice."

Meantime, Mr. Tresevant, after an impatient frown or two, had risen above himself and came forward to greet Jim Forbes. He did not offer to shake hands with him; he had not learned that art yet; truth to tell, he did not know the rough, young fellow well enough to venture, but his greeting was sufficiently kind, and Jim received it with an awkward attempt at courtesy.

"Mr. Forbes is going to Boston on this train," explained Dell. "So I shall have someone to take care of me."

Then there came over Mr. Tresevant a suffocating sense of the fact that he, being a minister of the gospel, ought to say something improving to this young man, and he said the last thing that Dell would have had him say if she could have chosen. "You must keep away from all such places as that which I saw you about to enter if you are going to take care of the ladies, my boy."

The "boy" blushed to the roots of his very red hair, but answered promptly enough, "That's easier said than done when there's one of them places at every corner, and folks hanging around to coax a fellow in."

"That is true," Dell said quickly. "But, Mr. Forbes, there is coaxing going on on the other side too, you must remember. Don't you know how much I want you to join our temperance society, and that, you see, would be a help to you as well as to us." Saying which, she looked wistfully at Mr. Tresevant, half hoping he would in this one case see the merit of a pledge and join his persuasion to hers. But Mr. Tresevant looked down at his boots and was gravely silent. As for Jim Forbes, he only blushed the harder and muttered, "I dunno about that." And then the train shrieked itself in, and in a very few minutes out again, taking Dell and her escort with it.

Dell settled herself into a seat and made room for Jim beside her; that gentleman, however, preferred the arm of the seat, and stationed himself thereon. Gradually Dell became unpleasantly conscious that she was attracting attention. She was very well aware that she was a neat, trim, becomingly dressed maiden; and she was equally well aware that Jim Forbes was a tall, ungainly, freckled, tanned, red-haired youth, in a very much soiled factory shirt, minus collar and cravat, and with a well-worn, not to say ragged, coat hanging on his arm; yet there he sat on the arm of her seat and talked earnestly to her. The stares became frequent, and some of the comments were loud.

As the train neared Boston there came in the Chesters, the three young ladies, and Mr. Will Chester; they were eager and joyous in their greetings.

"Why, Dell! Dell Bronson! What a delight to see you again. Are you coming home to stay? One week! How awful. Oh, Dell, we *can't* let you go away again." And then they turned wondering eyes on poor Jim, and Will Chester leaned forward and said:

"Isn't that fellow offensive to you? Shall I suggest his removal?" and Dell, flushing almost as deeply as Jim himself, answered quickly, "Oh, no; I know him very well," and turned again to Jim with a cordial, "Finish telling me about that evening, now, will you?" And the Chesters stared and wondered and whispered.

At the next station there came the De Quincys. Now the De Quincys had been in the habit of, well, not exactly turning their aristocratic heads away from Dell, because Mr. Edward Stockwell's niece was not a lady to be turned away from, even by the De Quincys, but they thought her "exceedingly peculiar" and were rarely in sympathy with her "singular" movements. They came over to greet her, and to assure her that Boston had missed her. And then Jim endured some fearful staring, and Miss Helen De Quincy whispered, "Is that dreadful creature intoxicated? Why don't you appeal to the conductor?"

"Because," said Dell, all her blushing embarrassment gone and her eyes brimming with mischief, "because I have no need of his services. The *gentleman* is a particular friend of mine." To tell the truth, Dell heartily enjoyed shocking the De Quincys.

At last the train steamed into the Boston depot; two minutes more and the tall form of Mr. Edward Stockwell was gently forcing its way through the crowd. Even the De Quincys stepped a little to one side to let him pass; there were very few who were not willing to yield to Mr. Edward Stockwell.

"Oh, Uncle!" Dell said breathlessly, with very bright, yet very moist eyes. And the voice, gentle and tender as a woman's, yet with a strange sense of strength about it, answered, "Darling child." And Dell knew that she was at home once more. She turned suddenly to her companion and spoke eagerly, "Uncle Edward, this is Mr. Forbes."

Mr. Stockwell's keen eye lighted with a genial smile. "One of your class," he said instantly. "I remember the name perfectly; welcome to Boston, Mr. Forbes. Thank you for taking care of my niece." And Jim Forbes felt his hand held in such a cordial, kindly grasp as he had never known in all his life before. And both the De Quincys and Chesters stared.

"Now," said Uncle Edward, as the train fairly stopped at last, "we can go, I think. One, two, three. Any more, Dell? Mr. Forbes, if you will take the traveling bag, I will manage the rest." And so Mr. Forbes made his first awkward essay in waiting on a lady.

"Where do you stop?" further questioned Mr. Stockwell as they neared his carriage. "Any place in view? Oh, let me direct you then, will you? I'll find you a very convenient place; just take a seat in the carriage. I'm going directly past where you would like to be. Oh, certainly get in; there's plenty of room. It's no trouble at all; a friend of Miss Bronson is a friend of mine." And Jim Forbes leaned back among the puffy cushions and wondered as they whirled through the streets what would happen to him next, and what Joe and Tom and all of them would think if they could see him.

At a certain point Mr. Stockwell stopped the carriage and sprang out. Entering the building where a dozen men were writing, he said briefly, "Mr. Lewis, I want to see Carey a moment." From an inner office a brisk young man was promptly summoned.

"Carey," said Mr. Stockwell, "Miss Dell has come, and in company with her is a young man from the country, one of those whom Satan tempts on every side. Can you get him in at your boarding place and help him through with his business? He is a very rough young fellow. Needs especially to avoid saloons and the like." The young man thus addressed answered in a tone prompt and energetic enough to be Mr. Stockwell's own, "I'll look after him, sir. Where shall I find him?"

"Here, in my carriage." Mr. Stockwell meantime drew his pocketbook and placed a bill in the young man's hands. "And Carey, have you some pleasant place of entertainment and employment for the evening?"

"Yes, sir; but I have funds on hand."

"Never mind, this will do for another time, then. Come to the carriage at once, please. Mr. Lewis, you will excuse Carey for the remainder of the day if you please. Now, Mr. Forbes," Mr. Stockwell continued, being now at the carriage door, "I have a friend here who will look after your comfort with pleasure. Mr.

Carey, Mr. Forbes. You return tomorrow, I think you said? Will you call at my office in the morning? Mr. Carey will show you the way. Good afternoon, and thank you again for your kindness."

"Uncle Edward?" Dell said, clasping her hands in an ecstasy of delight, as the carriage door shut them in together. "That is just splendid. How *did* you remember all about this boy and know what ought to be done for him?"

"It is part of my business, dear child, as an employee of my Master, to remember people's names and study their character, as far as possible."

"Uncle Edward, it isn't possible to help these boys in Lewiston; it is a little bit of a village, and I suppose Boston is a great, wicked city, but if they were all in Boston I could help to save them. There is not a living soul to help them. No one who has any interest in them."

"What has become of Mr. Nelson?"

"He would if he could," Dell said thoughtfully. "But, uncle, there is nothing to do it with."

"Then it is the facilities that you lack, not the living soul; and in regard to that, dear child, isn't God in Lewiston? and have you forgotten that he has facilities to work with that we know not of?"

15

THE REVIEW

Teach me thy way, O Lord.

DINNER again in the dainty Boston dining room, so fair and pure in all its details that the very sight of it all rested and soothed Dell's beauty-starved heart. After dinner they went into the back parlor, where they used to linger together on summer evenings. And Dell, mindful of how many times she had longed for that seat, went straight to that low ottoman, wheeled it in front of Aunt Laura's chair, and snugged herself into it; and Aunt Laura's left hand fondly smoothed the soft bands of brown hair, just as she knew it would, just as she had imagined the touch endless times during the long days of that past year. Baby Laura meantime trotted with pretty restlessness from one object of interest to another, stopping to bestow shy, wondering glances on the forgotten cousin's face. Uncle Edward had brought pen and paper, and occupied a table at the west window. When his wife frowned on the business implements, he said:

"Just a very little writing, my dear; I have brought it here because I can imagine myself visiting with you. We must make the most of Dell; it is only a week, you know. I shall be through very soon, and meantime you may talk or play as the mood takes you; it will not disturb me in the least."

So they talked—one of their long, sweet talks in the quiet twilight. By and by the twilight deepened; Aunt Laura and the baby Laura went away together, and Dell turned for company to the piano—her dear piano, for which her fingers had fairly ached during the year of separation. She touched the keys with a sort of tremulous eagerness, and soft, sweet, plaintive sounds filled the room; sounds that made the writer over by the table pause and raise his head to listen. Presently he hurried the last line to its close, shut his inkstand with a click, and rising, wheeled a large chair toward the piano.

"Now, dear child, the music is glorious, but tongues are aching to be used. Begin at the beginning, and tell me about the year."

Dell wheeled around on the piano stool and, leaning forward, rested her hand on his arm as she said:

"Oh, Uncle! The beginning? What a long story it will be! And yet after all there is just the least little bit to tell; it has been a long year, and I have tried to do a great many things, and I have done none of them. That, after all, is the whole story in a nutshell."

"But I don't want it in a nutshell. I want the whole story spread out, detailed; unless you have greatly changed, you know how to do it. Has Lewiston changed much? I haven't seen it in eight years, you know."

"Uncle, it has changed backward. It is the meanest, dullest, stupidest place I ever heard of. There is no paint on the buildings and no posts to the fences; they have rotted and tumbled over. And the church—oh, dear me! I can't detail that to you. Why, your carriage house would make a delightful house compared with it. And there is a rum hole at every corner. Oh, worse than that; some between corners. I never saw such a place."

"Yet the people are not poor?"

"Poor? No, indeed! There is wealth enough in the place to revolutionize it; but I don't know what is the matter with the people; they have no enthusiasm for anything but their stores, and factories, and saloons. Uncle Edward, what do you suppose God thinks of such Christians as there are in Lewiston?"

Uncle Edward looked up suddenly, smiled a kind, grave smile, laid a tender hand over the little one resting on his arm, and said:

"He has told you and me what to think about them; we must remember, 'Judge not, that ye be not judged; and with what measure ye mete, it shall be measured to you again!' What of the dear father, Dell?"

"Uncle, there is nothing to say. That awful tavern is still there, and Father is selling rum as usual, and— drinking it." The last two words with lowered voice and burning cheeks.

"And what is our darling doing for him just now?"

"There is nothing for me to do," she answered him sadly. "At least if there is I cannot find it. I have tried everything that I can think of and failed in all."

"Then you are not praying for him anymore?"

"Oh, Uncle Edward!" with a quick, startled look, "you know I did not mean that. I am praying for him constantly with all my heart, but that is all."

"Well, about the class. Are you encouraged?"

"Why, they come regularly, and they seem to like me; but as to any change in them I see none. No, I can't say that I am encouraged. I am very heavy-hearted. What good for them to spend an hour a week in Sabbath school if it doesn't influence their lives a particle?"

Uncle Edward waived the question. "Is Mr. Tresevant any help to you?"

Dell's eyes flashed. "No, sir, he isn't; he is a drawback. I have written you about Mr. Elliot? Well, I believe he could be gotten into our Society but for Mr. Tresevant's influence; he actually uses it against us. Uncle, do you see how a *good* man in these days can work against the temperance cause?"

"No, my dear, I don't. Yet I trust the Lord sees how they can work against some phases of the temperance cause, and yet be, not *good* men, perhaps, but Christian men. Understand me, dear child, I am not in sympathy with this man, who is now your pastor. I believe him to be mistaken; if he is, the Lord will someday set him right. But, in the meantime, you and I must remember that he is your pastor, and speak and think of him accordingly."

Dell laughed a little. "Uncle Edward," she said playfully, "don't you think it would be well for me to stop 'detailing'; don't you see that I have grown uncharitable?"

"Let me ask one more question first: What of Mr. Nelson?"

"He is the same mystery that he was at first; working faithfully, and apparently conscientiously, yet without conscientious motives. Indeed, Uncle, we are all just what we were a year ago."

"Is that possible?" her uncle asked quickly, with an earnest, searching look. "My dear daughter, I have asked many questions about others; will you answer one very carefully concerning yourself? You and I think that to stand still for a year is impossible. Have you, darling, gone onward? Do you find your faith stronger, your trust firmer, your heart and life more entirely hid with Christ in God?"

Dell's head went suddenly down on the arm against which she leaned, and her bright eyes filled with tears; he waited quietly, and presently she raised her head again and spoke earnestly:

"Uncle Edward, I don't know; sometimes it seems to me that I have gone backward. I have tried to work for Christ. I know I have that end in view, but in every single thing I seem to have failed. I have done nothing; it seems to me almost a wasted year; and there are times when I want to run away from it all and hide with you and Aunt Laura; and there are times when I am utterly impatient and rebellious and think that I have done all I can, and it is time there was some fruit. So a great deal of the time I am not happy, and yet I don't quite know what is wrong." While she was speaking, Aunt Laura returned and took the low seat which her husband drew forward, in front of him, and beside Dell. Then he answered the young girl's wistful look with a kindly smile as he said:

"Do you want me to pick your work to pieces, dear child, as I used to when you were indeed a child, and criticize it?"

"Indeed, Uncle Edward, I want your help. I have wanted it more than I can tell you."

"Then, my dear, I shall have to tell you that I think the main trouble with you has been a too vivid realization of the person called 'I.' I do not mean by that, that you are troubled with egotism. I do not consider that one of your faults; nor do I mean that you have too strong a sense of personal responsibility, but that your temptation is to forget that you are a worker with God. It is a temptation common to us all; you grow discouraged; you think your efforts have been failures. Now, there are two or three questions that you should carefully ask yourself. First, am I really engaged in a work in which I believe the Lord himself is interested? If so, is he discouraged; or has his working *with* me been a failure? That puts the failure in a very startling form, you see. Our own shortcomings we have reason to lament, not sitting down with folded arms using up precious time while we mourn, but with the only true sorrow, that which says, 'God helping me, I will not make that mistake again, or leave that duty undone tomorrow'; and then, giving a firmer buckling to the armor, starts out afresh; but to lament over the nonaccomplishment of a work, our part of which we have honestly and earnestly tried to do, is, in my opinion, forgetting the fact that when our part is done it is God himself who is to do the rest. You may depend upon it, dear child, that the Lord wants that dear father of yours, and Sam Miller, and Mr. Nelson, and all your class, to be numbered among his jewels quite as much as you possibly can; and he has ways and means with which to bring about his ends that you and I dream not of. You must drop that overtasked, much cumbered 'I' out of your thoughts, and learn to say 'We'; think much about the copartnership, tell it over often to yourself, reverently indeed, but yet triumphantly, 'God and I.'"

"But, Uncle, ought I not to feel a deep interest in, and—yes, in one sense—anxiety about these souls unsaved, in danger?"

"If you ask me whether you, if you be deeply interested in your work, will not be likely to feel more or less anxiety, despite every effort to quiet it, I answer 'Yes'; being a young, impetuous Christian, you will doubtless have much of this feeling to struggle with, but that it should be struggled with until we reach that more blessed resting place where we can say, 'It is the Lord, let him do what seemeth him good,' I assuredly believe. Don't you know the direction 'And having done all to stand'; and yet another, 'Wait on the Lord; be of good courage, and he shall strengthen thy heart; wait, I say, on the Lord'? We have many directions about that sort of waiting, Dell, and your eager heart needs to learn the lesson carefully." A little silence fell between them. Dell's hand sought Aunt Laura's and was firmly and lovingly clasped. Finally she looked up with bright, grave eyes, and said earnestly:

"Thank you, Uncle Edward; you have given me the help I needed."

"I think if you follow my advice you will find yourself rested; there is no more solemn prayer, and I think none more needed, for us who are called by his name, than that which our Elder Brother left among his latest for us: 'Not as I will, but as thou wilt.'"

Then a sudden change of subject. "Have you really decided, Dell, that you must not accompany us to the seaside; for a little rest, you know? We have counted on it very much."

Dell answered him with her old, bright smile and very earnest eyes as she quoted with peculiar emphasis: "'And having done *all* to stand.' There is work for me to do, Uncle."

And her uncle laid his hand on her head and answered solemnly, "The Lord, before whom I walk, will send his angel with thee and prosper thy way."

There were days that followed like flashes of sunlight, the beauty and joy and rest of which Dell never forgot. So unlike they were to the dull, shivery, rainy one in which she rubbed the car window with her handkerchief to catch one glimpse of the retreating form of her Uncle Edward as he drew his cloak about him and bent his umbrella forward to shield himself from the sleet, that she half wondered if the time that had seemed such a tiny week to her had not after all been months, and whirled her right into the middle of November dreariness. But it wasn't; it was only one of those delightful August foretastes of what November can do. Dell struggled bravely with her homesick, desolate heart; she tried not to think of the difference between Lewiston and Boston as the train shrieked into or rather by the side of the Lewiston depot, and she clambered out alone, and bargained for a seat in the mail wagon, and thanked a stranger for a piece of his umbrella. When she landed in the hall at home, which despite all her rearrangements looked dingy enough, she resolutely put from her the thought of that other long, wide, beautiful hall, giving glimpses through half-open doors of fair rooms on either side; and to her father's greeting, "Well, and so you are here?" she answered cheerily, "Yes, I'm here," and then she went straight over to him and bestowed a hearty kiss on the rough, red face. As she went up to her own room, she had need again to shut out comparisons and cheer herself with something. So she said, aloud and firmly, "Wait on the Lord; be of good courage, and he shall strengthen thy heart; wait, I say, on the Lord."

There had already ripened some fruit from that Boston visit, if Dell had but known it. Jim Forbes, walking down to the factory with his friend and boon companion Cooley, gave a detailed account of his Boston experience and finished it on this wise:

"Him and her, both, couldn't have treated me no better if I'd been a prince, and I'll tell you what my mind is made up to, Cooley. I'm going to sign that there pledge the very next meeting they have— blamed if I don't." And he did.

16

―――― ✦ ――――

PRINCIPLE OR EXPEDIENCY

But he knoweth the way that I take.

MR. TRESEVANT stood over by the mantel, leaning his arm on it and resting one hand on his head; his face was very pale, and his lips were pressed tightly together, as if he were trying to control some strong feeling. Dell sat in a low chair at a little distance, nervously picking to pieces a great pink rose, showering the leaves about the floor in reckless fashion. The pink on her cheek was deepened to a vivid crimson, and the hands that pulled apart the heart of the rose trembled visibly. When Mr. Tresevant finally spoke, his voice was low and constrained.

"It is a most singular idea of duty; one that I cannot comprehend. I trust too entirely in your truth to believe for a moment that it is a flimsy excuse, and that you are hiding your real feelings from me; but—is it not a very trivial question to come between us?"

"Not trivial to me, Mr. Tresevant. I thought you understood my position on this question. I have surely reason to consider it in a very solemn light."

"But, Dell, I do not interfere with your views on the question. I have even told you that I respect them. What more would you have?"

"But you are not in sympathy with them?"

"That is, I do not carry my ideas to the same length that you do. Surely, as a sensible woman, you do not require this of any man. I do not ask it of *you.*"

"I ask it," she said, with trembling lips. "On this one subject I ask it. I need it. I dare not do without it."

"Dell," said Mr. Tresevant, and there was a touch of bitterness in the sarcasm of his tone, "do you really consider me in danger of becoming a drunkard, because I do not deem it proper to sign a total abstinence pledge?"

His tone seemed to give her strength; she gave him the benefit of a full look into the depths of her great, earnest eyes as she answered, slowly and steadily:

"I do not consider even that impossible. I have known men as secure as you seem to be who have fallen victims. I do not consider any man absolutely safe who is not an absolute foe to liquor in all its forms. But it is not that phase of the difficulty that presents itself most forcibly to me. We are truly not in sympathy in regard to this thing. I have felt it keenly during the progress of our acquaintance. How much more sharply do you think I would feel it if my life were part of yours? There is another thing. I cannot feel that your views in regard to this subject are right. I cannot feel that God will bless you in them; you stand in the way of men who you know are in danger, even if you are not, and you do not put forth a helping finger; you even by your silence and example encourage them in their evil way. You do this very thing with Mr. Elliot; you must know that he is in danger, and you know what an influence you have over him; yet, how do you use it? And I look on and am powerless to help it, and sometimes it almost drives me wild.

How do you think I could endure it under other circumstances?"

"You exaggerate difficulties," he said, struggling with his own heart and trying to speak calmly; "it is your nature to do so; you are excitable, easily moved to extremes, and you see mountains where there are only molehills. Young Elliot, for instance, is safe enough; a little fast for a young man in his position, but I am doing what I can to restrain him and hope to succeed in the end. Indeed, I do not think I deserve to be judged so harshly as you are judging me. I am trying in my way to do good in the world, if it is not quite like your way. May not the Master own it after all?"

Dell's voice was very humble in answer. "I do not want you or anyone to work in my way. I don't want to choose my way of working. I have asked God to show me his way. It is not a method of work, but a principle, of which we are speaking now. I consider total abstinence from everything that intoxicates a solemn Christian duty. You do not think any such thing. Now Mr. Tresevant, how could we agree?"

"By agreeing to disagree. You have a full and perfect right to think as you do, and thinking so, are right in working to your views of duty. I accord this right to you. Cannot you do the same by me?"

"But can we both be right and both move in opposite directions? Is there then no such thing as an enlightened conscience guiding the *only right* way? If I choose to think that making calls and visits on the Sabbath is a proper thing to do, have I a full and perfect right to do so, and would you accord me that right?"

"The cases are not parallel in the least," he said, changing his position uneasily; "the one is a plain

Scripture injunction which we have no right to question, the other is at least only a difference of opinion."

"Now you have reached the very point where we should differ the most. I consider the one Scripture injunction as plain and unquestionable as the other. When I hear my own poor father quoting the fact that you drink cider, as an excuse for his business and his habits, can you wonder that I think the solemn declaration, 'If meat make my brother to offend, I will eat no flesh while the world standeth,' as binding upon Christians as that other command, 'Remember the Sabbath day, to keep it holy'? The first is not, it is true, in the form of a command; but should a Christian follow only commands, without regard to the spirit of the gospel?"

"That is true," he said gently. "But, Dell, the precise path in which a man should walk is not always marked out for him in the Bible; he is left to be guided by his conscience, and you *must* learn to think that those who differ from your peculiar views may be conscientious in doing so. Perhaps," he added, with a sickly attempt at a smile, "it may be part of your mission to reform me. I will try to be a faithful pupil, won't you take me in hand?"

But Dell could not control her voice to answer him lightly; a sudden mist swam before her eyes; she looked down at the rose leaves in utter silence. Her companion turned suddenly from his position by the mantel, pushed an ottoman just in front of her and sat down.

"Dell," he said, and his voice was gentleness and tenderness itself. "Dear friend, won't you think this all over again, and see if you can afford for a mere trifling difference of opinion to blast your life and mine; you have told me that you loved me, and surely I have offered you no mean gift, the strong, true, abiding love of a manly heart. I feel that I need you. I need your help and sympathy in my work. I believe that God would bless us in our efforts to work unitedly for him. It cannot be possible that you will let a very trifle come between us. Can you afford to be so indifferent to God's crowning gift, human love?"

The deep crimson glow went out entirely from Dell's cheek, leaving it marblelike in its whiteness. A vivid sense of the desolateness and unlovingness of her life rushed over her, a vivid sense of the fullness of love and care and protection that this strong human arm offered for her to lean upon surged in upon her. Why not let herself be so blessed? Why should she be shut out from this crowning gift of God? She trembled with the great longing to follow the pleading of her own heart. Why not? He was a good man, a Christian man; she did not doubt in the least. Why let this trifle separate them? It *was* a trifle surely. From the not distant barroom came sounds of drunken revelry, voices many and loud, some oaths mingling with the coarse words and laughter; her father's voice distinctly marked above the others came full upon her ear, loud and thick like a man half drunken. She shivered with pain; if all *that* could be banished from the world, what a father he might be! How many fathers—yes, and how many husbands might be saved! Yet here was this man sitting before her, his pale, pure face looking anxiously into hers; this man, who was almost her promised husband, thought the temperance movement throughout the land a misguided sort of fanaticism; thought that men might be educated to a moderate Christian use of liquors, as of many other things that became improper if indulged in without restraint. Should she, whose life was pledged for a hand-to-hand struggle with what she believed to be the monster evil of the world, link that life with such lukewarmness as this? She drew a long, heavy sigh, then, bending slightly forward, spoke with the tremulousness of suppressed emotion, not of indecision:

"Mr. Tresevant, I feel to my very soul the honor you have done me. I have given you proof of that, in that I have confessed to you that my heart answers, as—as my conscience will not. My life is pledged to a certain work in which you do not believe; I feel that I could not do that work which I have promised God to try to do, if I became your wife."

"It is incomprehensible to me," he said in a low, placid tone, after a few moments of utter silence; "it is incomprehensible to me, if you feel toward me what you profess, that you can let this strange chimera come between us."

She looked at him searchingly, and after a moment spoke, timidly, "Is it any stranger than that you, professing to think *almost* as I do, should not be willing to yield one inch of your views to help me in what is such a solemn, terrible thing to me?"

Mr. Tresevant pushed his seat back with a sudden jerk; he was not a meek man by nature; he had been greatly humiliated that evening; he had been keeping himself under control for the past two hours. He spoke quickly and bitterly:

"I will not be forced into signing a pledge for any woman on earth, not even you."

A perfect shower of rose leaves torn in tiny bits fell at his feet, and Dell sat erect, and with clear, steady eyes looked into his. She was not meek by nature either, not she; and she had the advantage of him in that she knew he stood on the weaker side and could not argue even to his own satisfaction in favor of his position. Her voice was clear and firm. "Then, Mr. Tresevant, we seem to understand each other. I can only repeat what I have told you before. I can never marry a man who will not array himself on the side of God and humanity, in fighting against this awful wickedness."

Mr. Tresevant arose without another word, walked over to a side table and possessed himself of his hat, then came back to Dell and spoke in low, husky tones, "Good-bye," to which he received no answer, and seemed to expect none, for he turned away and went swiftly out at the open door and down the street.

As for Dell, you think she leaned her head on the window seat and shed hot, bitter tears. She didn't; such was not her nature. She looked at the fastenings of the blinds, drew down the shades, turned on the flame of the lamp a little more, noticing for the first time that it smoked. Then she went to the kitchen and gave her directions to Sally about the morning meal, as composedly as if she did not realize that she had just put from her the dearest and best thing that earthly life could ever offer her; stopping on her way back to see that her father's room was in complete and dainty order.

Arrived at her own room, she locked herself in, turned down the light to the lowest point that its smoky propensities would tolerate, and sat down to look the events of the evening squarely in the face. Nonetheless for her outward composure did she carry a very heavy heart. The long, blank future stretched out dully before her; she had turned away from the joy and blessedness that were held out for her. She realized in all its fullness what she might have been. She was not sorry for her evening's work, not in the least; she had nerved herself for the task; her words had not been spoken under the impulse of the moment; they had been carefully and painfully and prayerfully gone over when she saw that this question was to come to her. A little lingering hope there might have been that Mr. Tresevant's prejudices were not so deeply rooted as they had seemed; that he was more in sympathy with her work than she had thought, but never an instant's hesitancy as to her duty in the matter, except during that one breathless moment down in the parlor. That was all past; she was very quiet, not regretful; she had asked God to show her the right way, and she believed fully and firmly that he had; so there was nothing to regret. But she could not help thinking that threescore and ten was a very long time for people to live; she even wondered sadly what those people did who had to live seven, eight, and nine hundred years in the olden time. She was thankful that no such lot would be hers. There was a great deal of work to do, and she must not shirk it; but when it was all done, or, better still, if the time should come soon of her to leave it all, come through no seeking of hers but because the King wanted his daughter at Court and called her home, how pleasant it would be. She had no tears to shed; her heart felt too heavy for tears; but she took her one unfailing friend, her little, well-worn Bible, and turned its leaves rapidly; no loitering tonight over precious verses here and there. She knew what she needed tonight and turned straight to it.

"God is our refuge and strength, a very present help in trouble." She felt herself in trouble. She had asked to be led; she felt that God was leading her; she did not murmur, but the way he had chosen for her feet seemed very hard.

17

LITTLE MAMIE'S DEATH

How unsearchable are his judgments,
and his ways past finding out.

ALL day long had Dell Bronson been in and out of
Sam Miller's home; moving with that quick yet soft
tread which betokens that there is much to do, and
need for that sort of quietness that prevails when a
solemn stranger is being entertained. She had spent
much time there during the last three days. She came
in now bearing a host of white flowers and went with
them to the inner room. Mrs. Miller followed her, and
the two stood together looking down on little Mamie.
The child had never lain in so beautiful a resting place
before, and surely no sleep could be sounder or
sweeter than that which held the eyelids closed and
wreathed a faint, pure smile around the quiet mouth.
Little Mamie had suffered her last stroke for the cause
of rum. She would never shiver and pale again, because of her father's unsteady step. In her little delicate
coffin she slept undisturbed. Dell showered the flowers over her, placed a tiny white bud in her little waxen
hand, then stood waiting in pitying silence while the
poor, desolate mother studied through blinding tears
the features of her lost darling.

"She is too sweet to be put in the ground," she moaned. "Only see what a smile on her face, and she holds the flower just as though she was looking at it when she dropped asleep. Oh, I can't have her buried in the ground! Oh, Miss Bronson, she is too sweet and pretty for that."

"She is not too sweet for heaven," Dell said tenderly. "You must not think of her as buried in the ground; you cannot imagine how beautiful the place is that she has gone to." But Mrs. Miller's heart was too sore for comfort.

"I wanted her to live," she sobbed. "I needed her; I knew she could do what I couldn't. She was fond of her father, Miss Bronson, you can't think how she loved him, and he loved her too; folks needn't think he didn't, for he did; he was like a lamb with her always, when he was himself, and she could coax him to do most anything she wanted him to. She had begun to coax him to go to them temperance meetings of yours, and, Miss Bronson, you know he went once; and I know she could have got him over on the right side if she could only have lived, but now he'll go to ruin faster than ever; and God knows I wish I was dead and laid in the coffin with my darling." And then the great, scalding tears burst forth afresh and dropped on the waxen face before her. So natural the little one looked that it seemed that she would put her hand to wipe away the tears. What was there for Dell to say? The way looked dark enough, certainly. The mother's one comfort in life had been her fair-haired, sweet-faced, gentle-voiced Mamie. And Dell knew how, aside from all the deeps of love that the mother heart lavished on her one lamb, there was always the hope that the father would be won over from his evil ways by this child. He loved her. Dell, who had seen them often together, did not in the least doubt it. And now, nothing seemed more probable than that, stung by terrible remorse, goaded by every separate blow that he ever let fall on the frail baby, stung especially by those last blows only the night before Mamie was taken sick, he would plunge recklessly into drink to drown his wretchedness. It was a dark, dark way. She could not wonder that the poor mother wept and moaned over this open coffin, refusing to be comforted. There was but one ray of comfort; she returned again and again to that.

"But, Mrs. Miller, think—you have not lost her; she has only gone a little way, and isn't it good to remember that she will never suffer anymore? You know," this last spoken hesitatingly, for she knew she was treading on sensitive ground, "you know she had a great deal to suffer here, and that is all over now. No more pain or trouble of any kind for little Mamie."

Mrs. Miller rose up from her crouching posture beside the coffin and dried her eyes while she spoke rapidly, almost fiercely:

"You don't understand, Miss Bronson; you didn't know my Mamie as I knew her. She would have borne every thing that she did, yes, and a great deal more to save her father; that was her one thought, day and night. I don't understand it at all. I try to; I tried to take in what you've said to me about God hearing our prayers, and I've tried to pray; the other night I prayed all night long to him to save my Mamie's life, for her poor father's sake; and it all did no good. Here she lies, dead; and her father will go to ruin. I suppose it must be so; but I can't understand it. I can't believe that she will be happy up there in heaven when she looks down and sees her father and mother miserable. She loved us so, you know."

Poor, mourning mother! She had built her hopes on this fair bit of clay that lay motionless before her, and now she had nothing to which to cling. Dell stood looking at her with great, sad eyes, uncertain what to say, or whether it would be well to say anything. At last she ventured timidly, "Mrs. Miller, there is one verse in the Bible that comforts me more than almost any other: 'His ways are not as our ways,' it says, and I think of that constantly; when I make plans and God seems to come in between them and brush them all away, then I remember that he can certainly plan better than I; and that he wants the people whom I am trying to help. Wants them for his own, you know, a great deal more than I possibly can, and that quiets me."

Mrs. Miller only dimly understood her meaning. She knew nothing of the abiding trust that lived in Dell's heart; but she knew that Dell's father was in the same awful snare as her husband, and she knew that Dell's heart was heavy over it. She had come to understand the young girl during these months; they were waging war against a common foe, and while she worked for her father, Mrs. Miller knew that she still had given time and thought to Mamie's father; thus it was that she had let this girl dress little Mamie for the last time, and lay her in her coffin bed, and cover her with flowers.

Everything was done now, and already the people were beginning to gather to the funeral, so Dell drew the poor mother away. What a pitiful thing it was, yet what a wonderful thing, this human love! Here was this mother looking her last on her one treasure, her only child, yet mourning chiefly even then for her husband, who had as surely been the means of placing her thus early in her narrow bed, as though one of his cruel blows had sent her suddenly to join the dead. The house had been very neatly and even tastefully arranged. Dell had tried to give it as little as possible the appearance of a drunkard's home. The burden was heavy enough to bear without exposing the wounds more than was necessary to the outside world. The people were few and scattering who came to little Mamie Miller's funeral. Miss Emmeline Elliot led the choir, but she did not come; neither did the choir; but the mother had said only a little while before, "Couldn't they sing a hymn, do you think? Mamie loved to hear singing so much." And Dell had answered, unhesitatingly, "Yes, they would sing a hymn." So now she looked about her, somewhat startled to find that no choir appeared. It was the usual custom, she knew, in Lewiston; it had not occurred to her that they would not be likely to come, because it was only Sam Miller's child. So when, after much looking about her and much questioning of Tommy Truman, she began to understand the matter, she turned with flashing eyes to Mr. Tresevant. She had not seen him, save from the pulpit, since that evening when he bade her good-bye, three weeks before. But she spoke to him at this time, as though she had seen him but yesterday, "Mr. Tresevant, Mrs. Miller wishes to have singing."

"I don't know how to manage it," he said, looking troubled. "If I had known it before, I would have tried to induce some of the choir to come, but there is not one of them here."

"I can manage it," Dell said briefly. "I will sing."

"Will you wish to sing entirely *alone?*" he asked her, in a startled way.

"No," she said, looking past him toward the doorway, where someone was entering, "Mr. Forbes will sing with me."

Now it chanced that Jim Forbes, mindful of his old friendship for Sam Miller, and of sundry red-cheeked apples that he had given little Mamie, thereby winning himself to love her, had asked and obtained an hour's leave of absence to attend the funeral. And it also chanced that Dell, sitting beside him in Sabbath school, had occasionally heard him burst forth into splendid song, so now she went forward at once to claim his assistance; he was startled and confused and gratified all in one.

"But, Miss Bronson, I can't sing anything that you can," he said, blushing fiercely.

"Then I will sing something that you can," she answered quickly. "You can sing, 'There is sweet rest in heaven,' for I've heard you. Well, we will sing that."

"But," said Mr. Tresevant, on being informed of the selection, "do you think that will be quite appropriate for so young a child?"

"Yes," said Dell, with stern eyes and firmly set lips, "entirely so; if anyone ever needed rest from the heavy burdens of life, it is poor little Mamie."

So it came to pass that never was a sweeter and tenderer requiem more sweetly sung than that which floated around Mamie Miller's coffin. But Dell tried in vain to soften the despairing feelings in her heart and find appropriateness in the services that followed. "The Lord gave, and the Lord hath taken away; blessed be the name of the Lord!" quoted the clergyman; and Dell thought of the bruises and scars all over the poor little body and felt rebelliously that *rum* had taken her away. When he talked of the providence of God, she thought drearily of the bottle of rum in Sam Miller's closet; in vain she tried to make the service seem other than sacrilege; her faith was strong enough to grasp the thought that dear little Mamie was at rest, but it seemed to her overwrought heart that it was the earthly father's cruelty, not the heavenly Father's love, that had taken her from earth. Very dark looked the world. Sam Miller's heavy, half-averted face and bloodshot eyes, and the bowed mother's look of absolute despair, were alike suggestive of gloom and hopelessness. And the clergyman's smooth, gentle tones, as he dwelt upon the great army of little children redeemed unto God, jarred painfully; the little children were safe and glad. Yes, she believed that, but the fathers, such as these, who had abused their trust and made it impossible that their little ones should stay with them, should *they* be soothed to rest and sleep by the words of peace? Ah me! Dell was down in the depths, where so many Christians often fall. She had lost sight of the thought that in spite of the woe and want and wickedness and weariness of this wicked world, God reigns.

Well, the very small procession followed Mamie to that little grave under a maple tree, and the father bit his white lips until the blood came on them, and the mother moaned in the very bitterness of desolation as they lowered that tiny coffin, and the minister's calm voice said, "Earth to earth, and ashes to ashes, and dust to dust"; and then they went back to the dreary house, the father and mother and Dell. All the rest went away to their work, to their study, to their play; but Dell came back and set the chairs in less formal array, and drew up the paper shades, and put away in a little box one small wreath that had lain on Mamie's breast, put it with a curl of hair and a little speck of a locket that Mamie had worn and loved; and made a cup of tea and bit of toast that the poor mother could not eat.

Finally, she must go home; they would have to take up their burden of living alone. She could not help it; there was no excuse for longer tarrying. Out on the gate, through which she would have to pass, leaned Sam Miller. She was sorry for that. The stricken mother might have pity in her heart for him, but Dell felt little; her heart was bitter toward him. She did not want to meet him or speak to him. He held open the gate for her to pass, and as she was doing so, swiftly and with a silent bow, he stopped her.

"Miss Bronson, I suppose your father can do without me tonight?" he said hesitatingly.

"Yes," Dell said, he would not be expected that night.

"There was something else," he said, as she was moving on. "I think—I mean—will you tell your father that he will have to get someone else to do his work after this? I can't come there anymore."

Dell turned eager, hopeful eyes upon his face. "I am so glad to hear you say so," she said earnestly. "I have been hoping you would find better work. Where are you going?"

"I don't know," he said, with a grave, determined face. "I haven't got to that yet. I only know what I ain't going to do, and I'll tell you what that is, Miss Bronson, because I think you will be glad to know. I ain't going to touch another drop of rum, so help me God. I promised my little Mamie that, when I was all alone with her a few minutes the night before she died, and I mean to keep the promise. My wife don't know anything about it yet, but Mamie knows, and God knows."

It was impossible to give you an idea of the solemnity of Sam Miller's tones; they impressed Dell with a sense of respect such as she had certainly never felt before for him, and also a certain sense of awe, as if he were being sustained and strengthened by some unforeseen power. She held out her hand to him, having no words to say; he grasped it eagerly and then asked in a very quiet, determined tone:

"Have you got your pledge-book about you, Miss Bronson? I mean to sign the pledge, and I'd like to do it tonight, partly because I shall feel stronger after it's done and then—I think Mamie would like it."

"And your wife," Dell said, as she drew forth her unfailing pocket companion, a tiny black-covered pledge-book. "Why, Sam, only think what a world of comfort you are going to bring to her sad heart tonight!"

"Yes, it will comfort her; Mamie thought of that, too; she planned that I should tell her after we came back from *her* grave!" Then he rested the little pledge-book on the post of the gate and wrote with steady hand the name "Samuel Miller."

Home through the deepening twilight sped Dell. Home, and up to the quiet of her own room; her heart was in a tremble of thanksgiving and self-reproach. How utterly she had distrusted her Father; with the very weapon which she in her wisdom had felt sure would destroy, God had spoken to the soul in danger and turned his footsteps. And Dell sought her knees in thankful and repentant prayer.

18

SIGNING THE PLEDGE
THE SECOND TIME

My son, give me thine heart,
and let thine eyes observe my ways.

JIM FORBES had taken even less pains than usual with his dress—his coat was out at both elbows, and very much frayed and soiled at the wrists—and he loafed along in a reckless fashion, as though he knew he was looking his worst and didn't care. His companion was fresh and dainty in a newly ironed blue and white muslin of delicate pattern, soft filmy laces at throat and wrists, and a spray of mignonette shedding faint perfume all about her. The conversation on her part was earnest; with him it partook of his general appearance and seemed reckless.

"When a fellow has give up—why, that's the end, and there's no more use of talking. I tried it—you know I did—and it was no kind of use, and now I've just give up."

"But, Mr. Forbes, I don't believe in any such doctrine, you know. I want you to try again. No one ever accomplished much with once trying."

"Once!" he repeated fiercely. "I've tried a thousand

times. You don't know anything about it, Miss Bronson; no woman don't. I thought I'd rather cut my hand off than to break that pledge, and now I've gone and done it, and there's no use in talking."

"Let's act then, instead of talking," Dell said in her briskest tone. "You come right down to the temperance meeting with me and sign the pledge over again; then everybody will see that you are in earnest."

Jim shook his head emphatically. "No, ma'am, I ain't agoing to do it; whatever I be, I ain't the fellow to make promises and go back on 'em and make 'em over again as easy as that. I don't go over all this trouble again for nobody."

"Then," Dell said, with a weary sigh, "you will disappoint me sadly. I trusted you—I was not certain that you would get along without failures—because I know about the fearful temptations to which you are exposed, although you think I do not. You seem to forget where I live, and who my father is; but I felt confident that you would try again."

Jim Forbes looked down at the sad, young face with a sort of respectful curiosity in his gaze. "I'd not disappoint you if I could help it—I'd rather be hung than do it," he said at last, with a rough attempt at gallantry; "but you see how it is—I can't be anybody—and I ain't going to pretend I can."

"Mr. Forbes, won't you try once more, to gratify me?"

"And s'posing I do, and fail again?" he said abruptly, a half-determination expressed in his eye to do both the trying and the failing immediately, and so afford proof of his inability to be anybody.

"Why, then," said Dell promptly, "I should want you to try again." Whereupon Jim laughed; his bitter spirit was not entirely proof against her fresh, brisk tones and words. "Besides," she said eagerly, trying to follow up her advantage, "it is such a wretched time now to desert the field—just when you are needed. Don't you know Sam Miller needs your help?"

"My help!" snorted Jim in his most scornful tone, all the bitterness returning. "Jolly help I'd be to any poor wretch. And whose help do you s'pose I need to keep me straight, while I'm helping others?"

"God's," said Dell, simply and reverently.

To which he made no sort of answer; he had long ago ceased sneering at that name, at least in Dell's presence. They walked on a few steps in silence. Meantime, Mr. Tresevant and Miss Emmeline Elliot passed them, and Dell, intent upon her work as she was, had time to notice the weary, pale look on the clergyman's face, and to indulge one sharp pang of pity over the desolation of both his life and hers, ere she turned again to Jim and asked her earnest question:

"Won't you make another trial, rather than disappoint me, Mr. Forbes?"

"I can't do it tonight," he said doubtfully. "Why, Miss Bronson, you don't know the whole. You wouldn't want me to if you did. I—I"; he lowered his voice and his face turning very red; "I've been drinking, this very night, and all the fellows know it; and if I should go down there, anybody who stood near me would smell rum, and you see how that would look."

"I know all about that," Dell said calmly. "I knew you had been drinking when I first met you. I knew you were on your way to drink more. Do you think people who have been drinking liquor ought not to go to a temperance meeting or make up their minds to sign a pledge? I'm sure they are the very people I am after. As for the breath, I have my pocket half full of cloves; they will destroy the smell of whiskey. Mr. Forbes, will you go with me this evening?"

"Yes," said Jim, with a sudden determination gleaming in his eye, "yes, I will, I *vum.*"

They were very near the church now, and at the door Jim halted. "You go on in," he said gruffly. "I'll come pretty soon."

And Dell, deciding that to be her wisest course, left him. A very respectable audience was gathering. As literary entertainments the temperance meetings were growing in favor. Dell was at the wheezy organ, playing an interlude during the second song, when Tommy Truman made his way to her side and began an eager story:

"Jim Forbes was on the steps, but he would not come in; he has been drinking," Tommy whispered in low, shocked tones. "And he is ashamed; he says all the fellows know about it, and they are coming tonight, and he can't."

Meantime the organist prolonged the interlude, striking chords at random and questioning the troubled little speaker. When she began to sing again, she skipped two verses, sang the last, then passed down the aisle out into the hall. Jim lounged in a miserable state of indecision and shamefacedness against the door. She went toward him immediately, speaking rapidly:

"See how much you disarrange our programme by your tardiness. I had to skip the opening song, and put the second one third, because I didn't want to sing it without your bass. Do come in now; it is nearly time for the next singing."

"Miss Bronson—I can't—I vow I can't," said miserable Jim. "You don't know how I feel, and all the fellows are coming. It's no use talking."

Dell turned and looked full in his face with great,

solemn eyes and with unutterable amazement in her voice. "Why, Mr. Forbes, you promised!"

He returned the look, his very hair seeming to grow redder, and at last he muttered, "So I did, I vum! Well, Miss Bronson, I'll come," which he presently did, looking flushed and uncomfortable.

Mr. Tresevant, notwithstanding his settled and unwavering objections to the temperance pledge, seemed inclined to haunt the temperance meetings; he and Miss Emmeline Elliot were together this evening, and Dell wished at least one of them elsewhere.

When at the close of the literary exercises, Mr. Nelson asked for the forgiveness and reinstatement of one of their number who had broken his pledge, but was again among them, repentant and ready to try again, and when, after the pardon of the Society was unanimously granted, poor Jim stumbled forward, summoning greater courage for his awful passage from his seat to the pledge table than he would have required to face the cannon's mouth, Miss Emmeline giggled and whispered to her companion loud enough for both Jim and Dell to hear:

"Here comes Miss Bronson's protégé again. Do you suppose they have him sign every time for effect, you know?"

But Mr. Tresevant made some inaudible reply and looked very pale and very grave; he had not reached the point where he could ridicule anything in the remotest degree connected with Miss Bronson.

As for Jim, he drew himself up with fierce, angry eyes and had nearly laid down the pen when Dell, bending forward from her seat by the organ, murmured low, "I thank you *very* much, Mr. Forbes," and instantly the pen was grasped again, and the crossed-out name was renewed.

"I think it is very remarkable that you succeeded in prevailing upon that poor fellow to come tonight," Mr. Nelson said as he and Dell walked homeward after the meeting was closed. "Do you know he utterly and emphatically refused me today, though I presented every argument and inducement in my power?"

But Dell was sad. She did not feel encouraged or hopeful; it was well to bear a hopeful face before poor Jim, if she could, but in truth her heart was heavy. "I don't know that it will be of any use," she said wearily. "He will probably break his pledge again and be in a worse state than before. I confess I have very little hope of him."

Mr. Nelson eyed her searchingly. "Are you going to desert your colors and lose faith in the pledge at this late day?" he asked her playfully.

"No I am *not,* by any means," she said, roused and excited. "I have all the faith in it that I ever had, and mean to work for it just as faithfully. But I never believed it could work miracles, and it seems to me there is almost a miracle needed in his case. His education, you know, has not been such as to make even a solemn promise very binding, and his temptations are many and peculiar. I think the pledge is better calculated to keep earnest-minded young men, those who have conscientious natures. I cannot help thinking that there is but one hope for poor Jim; if he had the 'Strong Arm' to lean upon, then his pledge would be kept; but, unfortunately, those weak natures are the very last to submit themselves to Christ, so that really I am as hopeless in regard to that as I am about the other."

"Do you think weak natures are less likely to be religious than stronger ones?"

"Much less. Don't you think weak people are obstinate people? I think they nearly always have a mistaken idea of their own strength, while a really strong nature is always conscious of how little his strength amounts to after all, and what infinite resources out of and above himself he needs to sustain him."

"It is a new idea," he said musingly, "but I am not sure that it is not a true one. I don't know which people you class me among, the weak or the strong," he added, laughing. "But I certainly have a very modest and limited idea of my own power of accomplishing anything."

"I class you among the people who are doing violence to their own consciences, Mr. Nelson. I hope you will forgive me for speaking thus plainly, but I do not understand you. I do not see how you can reconcile it with your nature to live only half a life."

"I do not understand myself," he said, sighing a little. "I sometimes feel greatly disheartened about it all. But, Miss Dell, if I had your 'Strong Arm' that you speak of to lean upon, I do not think I would descend into the valley of gloom as you and I seem to have done this evening."

"Then why in the world haven't you it?" she asked him quickly. "You seem to have a realizing sense of the power that it ought to exert over your life; you see very distinctly wherein I fail, when my weak, foolish heart gets the better of my sense and my faith. Why don't you set me a better example?"

He laughed a little at finding his reproof so suddenly turned upon himself, but seeing that she waited for an answer, presently said, "Perhaps I haven't your confidence in the ability of the 'Strong Arm.'"

"Oh, yes, you have, Mr. Nelson. I think you believe in Christ just as entirely as I do; the intellectual belief I mean; the only difference between us is that you do not choose to accept him as your personal Helper."

"But, Miss Dell, don't you see what an inconsistent being you make me appear? Wherein would be the consistency of such a belief?"

"I certainly do not know, Mr. Nelson. Won't you please try to discover wherein it lies?"

And as she said this, Dell mounted the steps of her own home.

19

THE WEDDING AND THE WINE

They would not walk in his ways,
neither were they obedient unto his law.

ESQUIRE BURTON'S house was aglow with light. It was decidedly the most pretentious house in Lewiston, and Esquire Burton's family, with the exception of Judge Elliot's, took the lead in the village. On this particular evening of which I write, the house was more brilliant than usual, and quite a brilliant company was assembled.

A wedding is pretty certain to call out all the elegance of which a family can boast, and this was the occasion of the wedding of the daughter of the house, Miss Laura Burton, and the bridegroom was Mr. Chester Elliot. Among the guests was Dell Bronson, rather, it must be confessed, to her own surprise. Dell had never been received with marked favor by the young people of Lewiston, partly because with the consistency of this present age, while it was perfectly right and proper to drink wine and brandy, it was not just the thing to associate on familiar terms with the daughter of a common rum-seller; and partly because the young people of Lewiston did not care to introduce into their society so formidable a rival as the rum-seller's daughter bade fair to be. So Dell examined the cards of invitation with somewhat astonished eyes and speculated as to why she was invited. The first query was answered when, on passing the Burton mansion later in the day, the front door suddenly opened and there rushed out an eager young lady, followed by a no less eager young gentleman, who stood looking on with watchful eyes while the young lady almost devoured Dell with kisses. The Winthrops of Boston, guests of the Burtons of Lewiston. She could imagine Miss Laura Burton opening her brown eyes in mild surprise over Helen Winthrop's delight at the thought of meeting Dell Bronson again. There was a certain blue silk dress at home in Dell's trunk that had never seen the light of Lewiston; it had ruches of soft, full lace around neck and sleeves, it was exceedingly becoming to Dell, and she was very fond of wearing it; besides, a wedding was such a pleasant place to go to, and they were so few in Lewiston. So, as I said, Dell Bronson was one of the guests.

It was quite a Bostonian affair on a small scale; there were four bridesmaids, of whom Miss Emmeline Elliot was chief, and her attendant was Mr. Leonard Winthrop of Boston. Dell laughed a little over the lady's evident satisfaction at this arrangement, and yet felt that it was hardly to be wondered at. Mr. Leonard Winthrop was certainly a man to be proud of, if one chose to manifest pride of that sort. That most interesting feature of bridal parties, the ceremony, was just concluded. The bride, a small "pink and white" creature, lost some of her pinkness during the said ceremony and was becoming pale and interesting. Everybody had kissed and congratulated her and told everybody else how lovely she looked, and how handsome the bridegroom was, and how solemn and impressive the ceremony had been, and then the tide set toward the supper table. Thither went Dell and Mr. Nelson with the rest. The supper table was brilliant and in excellent taste, and the guests in excellent spirits. Conversation in brilliant, detached bits flashed up and down the table, till a question of the bride produced a sudden lull.

"Will you pledge my health and happiness, Mr. Tresevant?" and her jeweled hand rested daintily on the wine glass while she waited for his answer. Others waited too; Dell, sitting within a few feet of them, felt her color come and go, and could almost hear the throbs of her own heart as she listened for his reply. Very pale and very grave was Mr. Tresevant, but his answer was prompt and courteous.

"It is a most unusual thing for me to make the slightest use of the beverage in question; but at a wedding, and invited by the bride herself, one can hardly refuse." He touched his glass to hers and raised it up to his lips; not a single drop did he drink—Dell saw that—she saw everything connected with this scene. But what mattered it that not a single drop touched his lips, when, so far as his influence was concerned, he might have drained the glass?

Mr. Nelson was invited next and quietly declined.

Miss Emmeline Elliot arched her eyebrows to their highest as she asked pointedly:

"Is it possible, Mr. Nelson, that your pledge will not allow you to wish a *bride* health and happiness?"

"By no means, Miss Elliot; let me assure Mrs. Chester Elliot that I wish her all the happiness this world has to bestow."

"Ah, but you don't do it in the legitimate way. I should accept no such wishes as that, sister Laura. Seriously, Mr. Nelson, do you believe it is wicked to take such a tiny little swallow of wine as custom demands, here at this private table among friends? If one were in a tavern now or some such low place where common people congregate, it would be so different. *Won't* Miss Bronson allow you to do even such a little thing for society?"

The insinuations in both these sentences were coarse and low, unworthy of Miss Elliot's beautiful lips, but Mr. Nelson answered her with imperturbable good humor:

"Miss Emmeline, I am engaged to deliver a temperance lecture in the schoolhouse at Pike's Hollow tomorrow evening; won't you please come out there and hear me? I don't feel like producing my arguments here before their time. Meantime, society must excuse me for my awful breach of conduct and allow me to continue the social bore that I have been for so many years."

The roses on Dell's cheek had been very bright during this conversation, but instead of looking annoyed, there was a mischievous light in her eyes, and they only danced the more brightly when Miss Emmeline, nettled into an utter breach of courtesy, answered sharply:

"Well, you certainly have my sympathy, Mr. Nelson. I pity any man who, in this enlightened age, feels himself tied down to some little boy notion as absurd as it is childish, about breaking a pledge."

At this particular moment, the waiter paused beside Mr. Leonard Winthrop's glass and prepared to fill it. Quick as thought, the gentleman's hand was placed over the glass, and his clear, high-bred voice sounded distinctly down the table:

"Not any for me, if you please. I belong to that daily increasing number of young men who have tied themselves down to the little boy notion of total abstinence. How goes the work here, Mr. Nelson—is it encouraging?"

Dell did not hear Mr. Nelson's answer. She was engaged in watching the scarlet flush that had mounted to Miss Elliot's very temples. Such an egregious blunder as that diplomatic young lady had contrived to make! Who could have imagined for a moment that Leonard Winthrop, belonging to the Winthrops of Boston, was a champion of that absurd and babyish fanaticism, total abstinence!

Meantime, there was one of the company who evidently had no such scruples. This was none other than the bridegroom. Again and again he filled and drained his glass, until others beside Dell and the Winthrops began to grow unpleasantly conscious of the fact that he hardly knew what he was about.

A return to the parlors, it was hoped, would break the spell, but Mr. Elliot was too entirely at home in his father-in-law's house to wait for an invitation to help himself at the sideboard, and too far under the influence of wine to realize his condition.

"If you have the least influence in that direction, I beg you will use it to prevent more open disgrace."

Thus said Mr. Nelson, as he stood for a moment near his pastor, and he inclined his head as he spoke toward Mr. Elliot, who, with flushed face and loud voice, was talking eager nonsense.

The pale face of Mr. Tresevant flushed slightly, and he answered haughtily:

"I must beg to be excused. I do not boast of sufficient familiarity with *any* gentleman to preach him a temperance lecture at the same time that I am accepting his hospitality."

Mr. Nelson turned abruptly away and sought Dell, who at that moment was standing somewhat apart.

"I am utterly out of patience with that man!" he said testily, and she answered quickly:

"What man? Mr. Elliot?"

"No, Mr. Tresevant. Of the two he acts the most like a simpleton. No one expects much wisdom from poor Elliot, especially when he is tempted on every side, as he is tonight. But only think of a minister of the gospel setting him such an example—actually drinking with him! and standing aloof from him now, composedly looking on, when a word from him might quiet the fire in the poor fellow's brains! Miss Dell, do you wonder that I have little faith in a religion that bears such fruit?"

Dell's voice and manner were very gentle in reply:

"Do you really think, Mr. Nelson, that it is *because* Mr. Tresevant is a Christian that he takes such a strange, one-sided view of the temperance question? Or is that the weak point in his character that Christianity has not yet overcome?"

Mr. Nelson's gloomy face cleared; he smiled down on the bright, earnest eyes lifted to his as he answered:

"I beg pardon. I spoke harshly, I presume. I have some faith left in religion after all; there are other exponents of it than the one of whom we have just been speaking. Shall I tell you of what you remind me just now? A verse in our lesson for next Sabbath: 'Charity thinketh no evil.'"

Their conversation was interrupted. The loud-voiced bridegroom came toward them, his tones at once loud and thick:

"Are you admiring my wife?" he asked, glancing at a fair-faced, smiling picture that hung near them. "That doesn't begin with one up in the library; she is the very cream of sweetness in that one. Ever see it, Nelson? No! Then come up and see it now—it was that I fell in love with; but you needn't follow my example, you know; too late for that. Come on, friend," raising his voice almost to a shout. "Everybody who wants to see the lady I fell in love with, in her prime, follow me."

"Let us go," Mr. Nelson said, in rapid undertone, to Dell. "The library is further from the dining room than the parlors are." Others joined them until quite a group gathered in the library, among whom were the Winthrops, Mr. Tresevant, and Miss Emmeline. The face which they came to study was fair and sweet enough to have been an angel's. Dell looked at it earnestly and tenderly; there was a troubled expression in the depth of the brown eyes that she had never seen in the original—a suggestion that the young girl had, at some time, felt a suspicion that there might be sorrow in this world somewhere, though it had never come to her. A tender pity for the gentle child-wife crept into her heart as she looked from the pictured face to the restless eyes of the husband. How near the very edge of the whirlpool of sorrow seemed this bride to her! Would not God in his mercy interpose to help her?

One of the company now discovered that the balcony afforded a delightful view of the rising moon, and thither half a dozen of them went to view the wonderful miracle of the fiery world. Dell lingered beside the picture, strangely moved and saddened by the hidden tears in those soft brown eyes. From the window came the sound of merry voices outside, loudest above them Mr. Elliot's.

"Winthrop, what on earth possessed you to grow so broad and so tall both at once? A fellow can't see through you, nor around you, nor over your head. Hold on though, I have an idea. I'll occupy a loftier position than you once in my life; see if I don't. Clear the way, friends, I am going up to get a nearer view of the sky." And as he spoke he vaulted to the delicate iron latticework that surrounded the balcony. It was a wild, brainless idea—no sane man would have attempted to poise himself in midair on an iron thread after this fashion, and yet a sane man, having in some unaccountable manner found himself there, would have caught at the iron pillar, clung to the lattice below, and saved himself in some way; but this man's brains were confused with liquor; he realized neither his folly nor his danger. It was all done in an instant of time—the unexpected spring, the dizzy pitch forward, and then the shrieks and wild rushing down the stairs of those who had witnessed the fall. Dell went swiftly and silently down to the bride. A confusion of cries prevailed below.

"What is it all?" the fair "pink and white" creature said, turning to her, and then there was plainly to be seen that look of vague trouble in the brown depths of her eyes. "Someone has fallen, they say; fallen where? Who is it? Where is my husband?"

In the midst of which appeared at the window Mr. Tresevant's face, deathly in its pallor. "Dell," he said in a low, clear tone, and Dell turned toward him, "take her away—his wife—get her into the other room, quick, we want to bring him through the hall."

Dell turned back. "Come with me," she said, speaking with gentle authority. "I will tell you about it." And the fair, young creature, easily led, allowed herself to be drawn into the little room opening from the back parlor, and nestled into a chair. She looked up with great, frightened eyes. "I know something dreadful has happened," she said piteously, "but I tremble so, I would rather you did not tell me now.

I'm afraid I am going to faint. I always do when I am frightened. Won't you just please to call my husband? Tell him I want him, and he will come. Oh, I am fainting."

And Dell, with a deep sigh of relief, saw that blessed unconsciousness steal over her face; she took the tiny creature in her arms and laid her on the couch. There was a physician among the guests, and for him she sought. He was not occupied, as she had supposed he would be, but came at once.

"We will just let her be," he said in answer to Dell's query as to what she should get and do. "It is the most merciful thing that could come to her; she will revive soon enough."

"Is there a physician with him?" questioned Dell.

"Yes, two of them by this time, and no need for either."

"Why?" said Dell, in awed and frightened voice.

"He is beyond their help. He struck his temple on the corner step, and when we got out to him was quite dead. There, Miss Dell, she is reviving; what shall we say to her?"

20

THE SAD FUNERAL

*Thy way and thy doings have procured
these things unto thee.*

THERE are those to whom we turn instinctively when the house is full of mourning. They may not be those who are counted among our intimate friends when all goes well with us; but when sudden sorrow and consternation seem as if they would overwhelm us, there are certain helpful souls who seem to know what, and how, and when to do; and to them we look. Such an one was Dell Bronson. She had not been intimate in the Burton family during their bright days, but no sooner did this stunning blow crush down upon them than she roused herself from the position of passive looker-on, and in that terrible night that followed not one in the house but learned how thoughtful, and helpful, and quiet Miss Bronson could be. So when frightened servants and anxious friends besieged Mrs. Burton with questions of what, and where, she grew into saying, with a sudden lighting up of her bewildered face, "Just ask Miss Bronson, will you? She can tell you where it is," or "I will consult Miss Bronson and let you know; she has looked after these things for me."

And Dell, finding herself useful, nay, actually necessary, stayed on and did all those numberless things that relatives and more intimate friends could not be expected to do, besides many trifles for the comfort of this and that one that no one else thought of doing. Also the poor little bride clung to her, seeming to find in her quiet strength something like a refuge in which to hide away. She would give little answer beyond pitiful groans to the various perplexing and torturing questions concerning this or that article of mourning, until Dell, seeing that they were driving her nearly wild, came suddenly to the rescue, asked two or three concise, low-worded questions that could be answered by "yes" or "no," and settled the points at issue. After that, they said when appealed to, as to what the poor, young widow would like, "Just ask Miss Bronson; she will find out for you; Laura seems willing to talk with her."

So it came to pass that Dell was much in the darkened room where the widow, who had been a wife for three hours, lay buried among the pillows; was there when Mrs. Burton came in and went toward her daughter with troubled face.

"My darling, Mr. Tresevant has called for the third time. Can't you see him now, just a minute? He will want to know your wishes in regard to tomorrow." The young creature roused herself and turned her wan, white face and great, sad brown eyes on her mother.

"Mamma, there is only one thing that I am particular about, and you can arrange that for me. I don't want Mr. Tresevant to have anything to do with the services tomorrow." Mrs. Burton stood aghast, and Dell paused in her task of bringing order out of the chaos of the toilet table and turned toward her.

"But, my dear daughter, what a strange idea! Quite impossible to carry out; he is your pastor, you know."

"That does not make the least difference, Mamma. I do not want to see him at all, and I will not hear him say one word tomorrow."

"But, Laura, why? What am I to tell him? You don't realize how very badly this will look."

"Tell him anything you like, and I don't care in the least how it looks. I am tired of looks. I don't care for anything anymore."

"I am sure I don't know what to do," said Mrs. Burton in despair. "Miss Bronson, do you know anything about this strange idea?"

"No, ma'am," said Dell, and her voice sounded hollow and unnatural to herself.

"Laura, dear," pleaded the mother, "you will not insist on this, I know; it will make so much trouble and bad feeling all around. If you had an intimate friend in the ministry it would be different; but Mr. Tresevant has always been so intimate here, and he was Chester's particular friend, you know."

Laura's white lips quivered, but she raised herself on one elbow and spoke more resolutely than before:

"Mamma, I am entirely resolved on this point. I never want to see Mr. Tresevant again. He was not a true friend to Chester; he had influence over him; he could have kept him from what he knew a great temptation, if he had chosen. There would have been no wine at our wedding but for him. When we talked the matter over and I objected, Chester appealed playfully to him that he should settle the question; he answered that we certainly had an honored example; that there 'was wine at the marriage in Cana,' and not one earnest word did he speak to help me. Do you think that I will have that man speak his empty words over my husband's coffin?"

"Oh, but my dear, you are beside yourself," eagerly argued Mrs. Burton. "Mr. Tresevant knew he had no right to interfere in your affairs; that was a gentlemanly way of saying so; and as for the accident, poor darling child, it was a fall; no one was to blame, no one could have prevented it—any gentleman might have had the same."

While she was speaking her daughter laid herself wearily back among the pillows, with a sigh so utterly heartbroken that it fairly choked her mother's words in pitying awe.

After a little silence the poor girl spoke again:

"Mamma, you might talk all day and you wouldn't change my mind. I am fully determined. Arrange anything else as you choose. I don't care anything about it; only remember, I will not have that man say one word."

Mrs. Burton went away in despair, and erelong Emmeline Elliot came in, her face and eyes swollen with weeping; she had not seen her sister-in-law before that day, but she had evidently come now to plead Mr. Tresevant's cause. The young widow listened, or perhaps did not listen, to the eager arguments and expostulating words, returning the invariable answer, "It is no use talking to me, Emmeline. I am fully determined. I told Mamma so."

Emmeline turned at last to Dell, with smothered sharpness in her voice. "Is it possible, Miss Bronson, that you uphold Laura in this cruel and unladylike thing?"

For an instant Dell's eyes flashed, and it required all her self-control and the remembrance of that crushed heart lying there among the pillows to help her to answer in low, quiet tones:

"I have not felt called upon to advise Mrs. Elliot on a point wherein she did not ask my advice; but if she had, I should have said, 'If Mr. Tresevant is in any way connected with this trouble, his own conscience must be weight enough for him to bear. I would not add to it.'"

Then she turned and went out of the room. It was but a few minutes when she was summoned in haste and dismay. Laura had fainted, and Emmeline did not know what to do with her, and Mrs. Burton could not be found. The doctor had come to make his morning call and followed Dell to the scene of trouble. The next hour was a very busy and a trying one; the frail, young creature was roused from one long, deathlike swoon only to sink into another, so like death itself that sometimes their hearts fairly stood still in terror. When at last the doctor left her in a more hopeful state, he sought the mother and delivered his verdict: Mrs. Elliot's nerves had sustained a great shock, her brain was in a very excited condition, and there was strong tendency to fever; it was, therefore, exceedingly important that her slightest fancies should be yielded to, that her wishes should not be crossed in any way. She must be kept quiet at all hazards.

Soon after that, Mrs. Burton called for a private conference with Dell and, with much circumlocution and embarrassment, made known to her that she desired her to communicate with Mr. Tresevant on the delicate subject. Dell shrank in pain and terror from the task.

"Oh, Mrs. Burton!" she said earnestly, "I cannot help him; it is not my place to do so, and I should not know what to say."

"My dear, I think it is eminently your place; you have been so constantly with our poor child since the accident, and you can represent to him her peculiarly nervous state and the fact that she shrinks from hearing his voice in the service, because of his intimacy with poor Chester." Mrs. Burton delicately ignored the fact that this was not the reason. "You see, Mr. Burton's position, as an officer of the church, makes it an exceedingly difficult matter for him to manage, and I am sure I should never get through it without blundering. Now, my dear Miss Bronson, *couldn't* you be persuaded to add this to your long list of kindnesses? I assure you we shall never forget how kind you have been to us. And you are so intimately acquainted with him!"

Meantime, Dell was thinking—she heard only a word here and there of Mrs. Burton's smooth, flowing sentences. She pitied, oh, so deeply and earnestly, the pale-faced, hollow-eyed young minister, who fairly haunted this house of mourning in his eagerness to be of some service. This added blow that was to fall she knew would be a heavy one; she longed to avert it; failing in that would it not be less hard to endure, coming to him from her, told gently, and with honest sympathy, such as she could give? Thus thinking, she let herself seem to be persuaded, received in silence Mrs. Burton's voluble thanks and assurances of never forgetting her, and went down to Mr. Tresevant when next he called. He came forward to meet her, gave her a cold, trembling hand, and then said eagerly, "Dell, isn't there *anything* that I can do?"

She shook her head. "Everything is done, I believe, Mr. Tresevant."

Then, by his next question, he precipitated the entire matter. "I wonder when I am to see Mrs. Elliot to make arrangements about the funeral? Can you find out for me? It is quite time I knew what is desired."

Straightforward frankness had always been Dell's habit; she knew no other way, so now she spoke quickly, yet with an undertone of gentle tenderness:

"Mr. Tresevant, they have sent me down to talk with you about this. Mrs. Elliot is half distracted; she shrinks from seeing anyone, you among others, and they want you to make arrangements with Dr. Carswell to attend the funeral."

"Dr. Carswell!" he repeated in a surprised tone. "I did not know he was a special friend. What part in the service do they wish me to assign to him?"

"They want him to conduct the entire service. Mrs. Elliot connects you so closely in her mind with her husband that she does not feel able to hear your voice, and they would like you to make arrangements with Dr. Carswell and attend the funeral yourself as a personal friend of the family."

Mr. Tresevant stood before her, dumb with wonder, and with a heavy pain at his heart. What did it all mean? A friend he had certainly been to Chester Elliot, but not more to him than to almost any other young man connected with his congregation. A little influence he had possessed over him certainly, but he hoped he had some influence over all his people. On that principle was he never to be allowed to bury his dead? There was some mystery about all this.

"Dell," he said appealingly, "what does all this mean? I don't understand it. Won't you explain it to me?"

Dell stood before him with downcast eyes and glowing cheeks; there were great tears in her eyes. She longed to flee her task. How could she further wound the heart that she knew well enough was aching now, with a bitter, unavailing regret? Yet she would not deceive him. She spoke in low, tremulous tones:

"Mr. Tresevant, you must remember that Mrs. Elliot has undergone a fearful shock and is not yet capable of thinking calmly. She associates you with her husband's condition on the night of the accident; she perhaps exaggerates your influence over him. Thus much she cannot keep her pitying heart from saying. And so just now it is painful to her to see or hear you."

It was a heavy blow; it quivered through every vein in this sensitive minister's body. Dell felt it all for him; she fairly longed to clasp his hands and lay her head upon his shoulder, and weep out her sympathy and her pity. But he didn't know her heart; he didn't see the unshed tears in those brown eyes; he was hurt to his very soul, and he was just as unreasonable as most other sensitive people are when something unexpected has stung them. Besides, he didn't in the least understand the young lady whom he had asked to be his wife. So he answered her in tones as cold as ice, "This is evidently your work, Miss Bronson. I hope you may be able to enjoy your triumph with a clear conscience."

The tears in Dell's eyes had no disposition to fall after that; indeed, they seemed to have burned their way back to their source. Talk of his being hurt; he would never have any conception of *how* he had stung her.

If, she said in her heart, *if he really, after all that has passed, knows me no better than to think I could do that—why, then, what is the use of talking to him at all.* So she lifted her eyes, stern now and dry, one instant to his face, then turned and left the room.

"Have you settled the matter satisfactorily, my dear

Miss Bronson?" questioned Mrs. Burton, with both eagerness and nervousness; the exceeding impropriety of a rupture with their pastor, at such a time and under such circumstances, was of all things to be avoided. Dell even then was jealous for his honor and understood him better than he did himself. She answered quietly:

"Yes, ma'am, he understands your wishes; but I think he would like to confer with you concerning the arrangements to be made with Dr. Carswell."

Dell knew he would be his own proud self before Mrs. Burton, and the sooner he talked this thing over with the solemn dignity which the occasion demanded, the sooner he would calm down. But she had been stabbed to the heart.

21

JIM FORBES'S SPEECH

I have seen his ways, and will heal him.

I haven't heard a word from him since he went away,"
Mr. Nelson told Dell as they two walked down the
street together toward the church; it was the evening
devoted to the temperance meeting. "I used all my
influence with Mr. Elliot to send some other fellow
and let us keep Jim here under our influence, but I
accomplished nothing. Jim happened to be the best
man for the sort of work that they wanted done, and
of course his well-being must not be weighed for an
instant against the press of work. I fear the very worst
for him; he has gone to a hard place."

He spoke in a troubled tone, and Dell answered him
listlessly, as one weary and discouraged:

"He could hardly do much worse than he was
doing here; he broke his pledge three times, you
know."

In truth she was both weary and discouraged; she
was beginning to feel that she had toiled all night and
caught nothing. Nothing accomplished! or, at the best,
such trifles that they might almost pass for nothing.
Six weeks had passed since that sad funeral, and she
had not seen Mr. Tresevant to speak with him during

that time. She had hoped so much from that painful time. She had imagined that her faith was strong and the way distinct. She had believed that, from the scenes of that solemn time, God meant to speak with force and power to the soul of this servant of his and arouse him to higher views and holier purposes. During all her sojourn in the house of mourning, while mingling her tears of heartfelt sympathy with the widowed bride, there had been an undertone of solemn joy in her heart, and she watched and waited for the hour when she should hear him declare himself led by the awful power of God to look at life from a different standpoint. This hope, rather this belief, bore her up during the trying funeral scene, when the pastor sat with white, suffering face, apart, and heard the voice of a stranger lead the service; her heart bled for him. "It is cruel," she said under her breath. "He *cannot* think I had anything to do with it; or if he thinks so today, he will not tomorrow when some of the bitterness is past. I would not have him endure this scene if any word of mine could have helped it." And yet underneath this feeling was that other one almost exultant: "The Lord whom he serves is leading him, is showing him just where he stands, and he is good and sincere and will come into the full light."

But tomorrow came and went, and Mr. Tresevant went steadily on his usual work, doing nothing more, only avoiding her, not seeming to desire even so much as a glimpse of her. Clearly he believed his public disgrace was owing to her; and clearly, too, he thought only of the disgrace, nothing of the soul gone down to sudden darkness, that his outstretched hand might have saved. It appeared in time that the disgrace was not much after all. People remarked how deathly pale

Mr. Tresevant was on the day of the funeral; and how well it was that he did not undertake to conduct the services, else he would surely have failed; then they added that he must have cared more for young Elliot than they had supposed, and then they turned to something else and forgot all about it. So the minister carried in his eyes, whenever he was obliged to meet Dell, a look of proud satisfaction that her scheme to humiliate him had failed, and she knew not what to think; everywhere her work and hopes seemed equally to have come to naught.

So on this particular evening, she spoke bitterly, almost indifferently, about Jim Forbes; she did not feel indifferent, only discouraged. Poor Jim had certainly been a discouraging object; he had signed the pledge and broken it so many times that she had almost lost her desire to have him sign it. Now for six weeks he had been away, sent by Mr. Elliot to help mend broken machinery at another mill, situated in a town if possible lower in the social and temperance scale than Lewiston. And Dell felt as hopeless concerning him as Mr. Nelson possibly could, even though she nightly commended him to the "Strong Arm" that she firmly believed was "mighty to save," and Mr. Nelson never did any such thing.

Tommy Truman met them at the door and came forward to them, indeed, with eager face.

"Jim Forbes has got back, Mr. Nelson," he proclaimed when he was within speaking distance of that gentleman.

"Has he indeed!" answered Mr. Nelson heartily, while Dell said not a word.

"Yes, sir, and he is coming to the meeting this evening; he says he has got something to tell the meeting."

Dell looked up to Mr. Nelson with a wan smile. "He wants to sign the pledge again, I suppose—poor fellow!" she said, still speaking listlessly, and then they went into the church. A fair-sized audience was already gathered; it was becoming quite the fashion to attend these temperance meetings, the music and literary exercises continuing very attractive. Mr. Tresevant and Miss Emmeline Elliot were present. Mr. Tresevant very rarely attended the meetings during those days, but some power had drawn him thither on that particular evening. Presently came Jim Forbes down the aisle, with steady step and a clear light in his brown eyes. Also, Jim wore a clean shirt and a whole coat that had been carefully brushed; his hair was combed with unusual nicety, and his collar was firm and white; altogether, Jim had never looked so well in his life. Trooping down the aisle after him came Dell's entire class, and after them a large delegation of some of the worst characters in the mill. They took their seats noisily, with expectant faces. Evidently an unusual interest centered around Jim Forbes that evening, though he could not have been in town more than an hour. He went directly to Mr. Nelson and whispered a few words; that gentleman nodded assent, and then Jim quietly took his seat, pausing only to grasp Dell's hand for an instant as he passed the organ. At the conclusion of the literary exercises, Mr. Nelson announced that their friend Forbes, who had been absent for several weeks, had a few words to say. Jim arose at once and came forward with an air of simple dignity that was new to him and became him well, and this was the speech he made:

"I don't know how to make a speech. I never made one; but I've got something I want to tell you; I told the boys if they would come down here with me tonight I would tell them something, and I wanted to tell the rest of you. You all know what I've been, and some of you know how hard I've tried lately to stop drinking. I wanted to stop. I meant to stop. When I signed that pledge, I thought I had drunk my last drop; but it wasn't so; the pledge helped me a good deal; I went without drink, after I signed it, longer than I ever did before since I was ten years old, but I was tempted; and you folks who have never drunk in your lives don't know what it is to be tempted in that way. I broke my pledge. I tried to make the boys believe that I did it for fun, and that I didn't care; but it wasn't so; I felt bad. I can't tell you anything about how bad I did feel, but I thought there is no use trying anymore, and so I give up. But I had a friend," and here Jim's voice broke a little, "and that friend came after me and talked to me and coaxed me, and wouldn't let me go to the dogs that time, though I seemed to want to bad enough. So I tried again, tried harder than I did before, and you'd be surprised at the lot of folks that wanted to ruin me, and how hard they worked for it, and how few there was seemed to care whether I was ruined or not. Well, the lot succeeded, and down I went again, and that time I was worse than before; but I had the same friend sticking to me, and getting me to promise to try again; and though it seemed to me of no kind of use, I did try, some weeks at a time, and then I tumbled back again; and one night when my boss came and made an offer to go to another town to work, I jumped at the chance, for, says I to myself, 'I ain't nobody and I can't be; I've tried as hard as a fellow could, but I was too far gone before I begun; so now I'll go away and I can spree it as much and as hard as I like, and there won't be anybody to feel bad nor to coax me, nor to care what becomes of me.' So

I went away, and before I'd been gone one day, who do you think I found was after me harder than anybody had ever been before? Why, it was the Lord himself, and he didn't let go of me though I tried to get away. I went into a rum hole, and he followed me and coaxed me out before I took a single drink. I told him it was no use. Says I, 'I've tried it again and again, and I ain't nobody and I can't be; now I've give up for the last time and want to be let alone.' And says he to me, 'Jim, that's just the trouble—you've tried "it," but never have tried *Me*—*never.* "It" is a good help, but you are too far gone; you want something stronger, you want something so strong that you can't get away from it; you want more than that, something so strong that you can't want to get away from it. Try Me, Jim—try Me.' And it kind of flashed all over me that was the solemn truth, and I just stood still there in the street in the dark, and says I, 'O Lord, I will.' And I did. And all the while I was to work in that mill, and going up and down those streets, and passing hotels and saloons and cellars by the dozen, he never left me a single minute—not a minute. I didn't even want to go into one of them places; I shrunk away from them; I hated them. I worked against them all the time. I didn't feel afraid I should go back to them anymore, for I could feel that the Lord had tight hold of me. And now I am his." Here Jim paused in his rapid, eager talk, and drew out his handkerchief and wiped away the tears that had been rolling down his cheeks; and there seemed to be need for many handkerchiefs around the church just then.

"I've just one thing more to tell the boys," he began after a moment, "and that is, if they really want to get away from the rum, or even if they don't want to and are willing to be coaxed into wanting to—he's the

Friend and Helper to come to. The pledge is good; it helped me. I love it and I'll work for it; but God is stronger than the pledge, and some of us need just the strongest kind of help that we can get. Oh, boys, come and try my Friend; you don't know anything about him, and it's little I can tell you—but I can feel it, and so can you if you want to. Now I want everybody to know," and Jim drew himself up with strange dignity, and spoke in very solemn tones, "I belong to the Lord—body and soul—I'm going to live for him, and work for him; but there's something of a great deal more importance than all that—he's going to live for me."

There was a solemn silence in the room for a moment after Jim took his seat; the boys from the mill were absolutely quiet and grave; they had been listening while one of their number spoke in an unknown tongue, and they marveled greatly. Mr. Nelson arose at last and stood for a moment in silence, then his touched and tremulous voice broke the stillness:

"Our friend has proved to us forcibly tonight that his help is in God. He said, 'Some of us need just the strongest kind of help that we can get.' I want to vary that statement a little and express my solemn conviction that all of us need just that kind of help, and that it is found alone in God. I honor the total abstinence pledge. I believe it to be one of God's chosen instruments of usefulness. I will work for it from this time with renewed energy and earnestness. But I have been slowly turning from my early bulwark, that man needed but to use the strength inherent in his nature to be what he would. I feel that I need God; and I hereby pledge myself and all that I have and am and hope to be to his service from this time forth. Let us pray."

"I thought you would be happy tonight," Mr. Nelson said gently to Dell as they walked homeward, "and here you are in tears. How is this?"

"I am weeping over my own folly," Dell answered, smiling a little through her tears. "Though I pride myself on being a daughter of the King, it seems I *cannot* trust him to do his own work in his own time and way, but seem determined to insist on choosing *my* time and *my* way, and when I fail, discouragement and depression seize upon me as if the cause were lost."

22

THE FIRE

And the Lord went before them by day in a
pillar of cloud, to lead them the way;
and by night in a pillar of fire.

IT was after eleven o'clock when Dell, on her way to her room, paused before the barroom door and, hearing no sound within, ventured to open it and peep in. Such a contrast as that room presented to the rest of the house, which had long since come under Dell's sway. Scrupulous cleanliness and order prevailed, and evidences of a refined and cultured taste were gradually taking up their abode in every room. Everywhere but in the barroom—there she never penetrated—the more utterly comfortless and forlorn and dirty that place could be made to look, the better pleased was Dell, and certainly the blundering boy who had present charge of that department was calculated to do her soul good.

On the evening in question, she peeped cautiously in. Six or seven loungers in chairs or disposed along the wooden settees, and every one of them asleep; the close, confined air, the smoking stove, and the smoking lamps, together with the intolerable smell of tobacco and bad whiskey, had been too much for them, and their snores were becoming every moment more distinct and determined. Seated just in front of the smoldering fire, Mr. Bronson, tipped back in one of the hard chairs, his slouched hat pushed to one side, was sleeping with the rest. How old and worn he looked! Dell had never seemed to see before how sunken his cheeks were, and how very gray he was growing. Wasn't it incredible that a man as old as he, and as tired as he must be, should prefer to sit sleeping in that hard chair in that filthy room, with such surroundings and such companions, when there awaited him a bed as soft and white and sweet-smelling as careful hands could make it? Every day the wonder grew upon Dell. Every day the house took on a daintier aspect, and her father seemed in a sense to appreciate and enjoy it. Oftener he came, and longer he lingered in the fair gem of a morning room that she had made for his special entrapment. Yet what did it amount to since he daily increased his capacity and his passion for whiskey, so that often he came in a half-drunken state and sat down in her dainty, cushioned chairs and profaned the purity of that fair room with ceaseless spittings, and even with oaths! All to no purpose looked the sacrifice of Dell's life; her father had set up an idol in his heart long ago, and every day he bestowed more of his heart's love on it. Every passing day seemed to make it more improbable that he would ever seek any other love; yet looking upon him, Dell daily said over to herself this unalterable promise: "I know the thoughts that I think toward you, saith the Lord; thoughts of peace, and not of evil, to give you an *expected* end." She shut the door softly upon that disgusting scene and went up the stairs singing softly to herself:

> *God moves in a mysterious way,*
> *His wonders to perform.*

Actually singing! and her father sitting in that
dreadful barroom in a drunken sleep. You see, she had
an *expected* end. She said it over aloud after she had
finished her voice of song: "To give you an *expected
end."* Dell had risen into a higher plane of life during
these passing months. With her, in a sense, hope had
been lost, not in fruition, but in expectation. Why?
Because of the promise; rather, the long chain of
promises, link after link of which she knew by heart,
and on each separate link she fed herself, reminding
the King daily, hourly, of his own words, and she knew
they were of more importance to him than half his
kingdom, and she knew his scepter was held out to
her—so now she just waited in daily expectation of
the end that she knew was to come. How? Ah, just that
she *did not* know. Moreover she had given up trying
to know. Not given up trying to help, you understand.
Not a bit of that; she held on to her end of the chain;
she spread her little traps and snares and looked
eagerly to see if her father would fall into them, and
wondered if that were to be the way that the end
would come; and when *he* chose one by one apparently to ignore her ways, she told herself earnestly that
his ways were not as her ways, nor his thoughts as her
thoughts. And realizing how infinitely higher and
better his ways must be than hers, she put her hand in
his and trod bravely on. Certainly this daughter of the
King had learned one lesson during all her time of
humble waiting, worth all the hours of discipline that
it had required—the lesson of patient, prayerful trust.
She went briskly about preparing for rest; the hour
was late.

But late as was the hour, she dived down into the bottom of an unpacked trunk in search of a thick wrapper, lined throughout with flannel, that she had determined should go with Mrs. Cooley's bundle in the morning. Mrs. Cooley was sick, and the winter was severe. Dell had been sewing all that day, getting ready some comfortable garments for the sick woman. It was part of this girl's method of preaching temperance, and it also belonged, perhaps, in a curious way, to the doctrine of retribution, that while the father sold Jack Cooley all the whiskey he would drink, the daughter struggled faithfully to replace some of the comforts to the wife and children that this miserable man swallowed daily.

Two hours after that, she was in Boston having a delightful talk with Uncle Edward, when she was brought suddenly back to Lewiston; and she sat up in bed with bewildered vision and startled ears. *What* had she heard to awaken her so suddenly? she wondered—only for an instant, then the sounds rang out again on the still, clear air: "Fire! Fire! Fire!" caught up and repeated from mouth to mouth. She sprang up and looked out on the village from either window; no sign of blaze visible to her, but people running toward the hotel, and then a vigorous pounding, and loud calls at their front door! One glance into the hall revealed the secret; it was full of blaze and smoke. It was the work of an instant to envelop herself in the woolen wrapper that she had been at such pains to find, then rush downstairs and draw the bolts to that front door.

In poured the men ready and eager for work. That next hour has always been a maze of bewilderment to Dell. She knew she worked; tore up and downstairs; brought blankets to wrap around Father and the six drunkards with him; she knew they were rescued at infinite risk, and that Sam Miller and Jim Forbes were foremost in the work; she knew that she brought keys and unlocked doors to save the time it would take to burst them open. Finally, she remembered coming downstairs with her Bible and her watch and Mrs. Cooley's bundle, and following her father across the way to Parker's. But all her movements were mechanical and unreasoning. In the course of time she realized that her father had been badly wounded; that he was lying on the bed, and that she was to take care of him. The doctor had been there and dressed his wounds and given him an opiate. While he slept, unconscious still of much that had been, Dell stood by the window and watched the men across the way, working like soldiers in a battle. And she saw plainly enough that in another two hours, there would not be a beam or a plank left of the old tavern. Even at that solemn hour a strange feeling of exultation came over her. No more whiskey would ever be sold there! Her father had drunk the last drop that he would ever get at that bar, at least. And then what barrels and barrels of the poison were being made away with, licked up by the wild flames! So much more reasonable it looked than to see men swallowing it.

Then again came to her those two lines:

> God moves in a mysterious way,
> His wonders to perform.

She did not sing them this time, but she thought them as she stood at the window and watched the house that had been such a curse to the village melt away. Presently she spoke aloud and solemnly:

"This is *his* way, is it? Well—*burn*."

Before evening of the next day, this young victim of rum had reason to feel that it was not all licked from earth by the last night's flames. Her miserable father lay on his bed, unable to move hand or foot, but able to speak, and the constant burden of his cry was "whiskey!" Burning with fever, suffering in every nerve, realizing that the ill-gotten gains of years had perished in half a night, this one desire was yet strong enough to overreach all other feelings. "Something to drink—something to drink."

In vain Dell tried all her dainty little arts of pleasing, prepared and brought this and that cooling liquid and held them temptingly before him; he wanted none of them, "Something strong, something to build him up," this was his constant groan. Everybody with whom she came in contact conspired against her. Wise ones gravely shook their heads and said it was wrong to cross him so; that he was accustomed to stimulus and he must have it or he would die. Even Mr. Nelson, who called in the course of the day, when Dell pitifully appealed to him for encouragement, said doubtfully, he did not know, he was sure; he was not skilled in these things; perhaps, as he had always been accustomed to it, it might be dangerous to irritate him so; yet he should very much dislike to give him stimulus if he had it to decide. But at the same time, it was hard to go contrary to everyone's opinion, physician and all. On the whole, he did not know anything about it; it would be impossible to tell what he would do if he were similarly situated.

Throughout the long, weary day, Dell stood resolutely on guard, resolute outwardly at least, but with such a troubled heart. What was the right thing to do? Could she possibly bring herself to give him a drink of that hated poison, after having spent so many agonizing hours in prayer for his release from its dominion? In the early evening they were having another debate on the same question—the dapper little doctor, who was Dell's special dislike, and herself—Mr. Nelson standing apart an interested and troubled listener, and Jim Forbes an eager and excited one.

"Now I tell you, Miss Bronson," Dr. Jones said pompously, "you can't make the world over in a minute, even if it would be well to do so at all. Your father has been used to a drink of whiskey every day, and whiskey he must have or he will die, as likely as not; anyway, this chafing and fretting are very bad for him; you can certainly see that."

"But I thought that whiskey was not considered advisable by anyone during a fever," said poor puzzled Dell.

"But, my dear Miss Bronson, the fever is doubtless the result of this day's constant fretting. I would not wish to overurge you, but really the consequences of this strange fancy on your part may be serious."

If only she could but trust him, could be sure that he knew what he was talking about; if only she knew what was the right thing to do! She looked wearily over in the corner where Jim Forbes stood; he stepped forward a little—his eager look attracted her attention.

"I wouldn't give him rum, Miss Bronson," he said earnestly. The little doctor wheeled around on him with an angry air.

"Perhaps you would be willing to undertake the case," he said with a haughty sneer.

Dell interposed. "I am not convinced that it is the best to feed my father on what has been his lifelong curse; until I am, I shall not give him brandy."

"Young lady, would you like to have your father die?" asked Dr. Jones, with tremendous emphasis and in his sternest tones, which truth to tell were not very stern, for dignity and sternness were not his forte. The thought, not the words, paled Dell's face. *Could* she have her father die as he had lived, drinking away his senses, lulled into his last sleep with that awful rum? And yet was her action periling his life? Poor weary girl, she seemed hunted on every side. A slight bustle in the hall arrested Dr. Jones's attention. Dell had not noticed it, but when the door opened she raised her eyes. A tall, handsome form, a gentle, manly, trustful face—one glance and then Dell sprang forward with something between a laugh and a sob, exclaiming:

"Oh, Uncle Edward! I knew you would come."

"My darling," he said in that voice of father sweetness and tenderness; then, "How is he tonight?"

And Dell held up her head and her thoughts went back to her father. "He is worse, I am afraid, Uncle Edward; must I let them give him brandy?"

"We will try to determine that very soon. My dear, do you see my companion?"

He was a tall, grave, gray-haired man; he stepped a little out of the shadow, and Dell's face lighted with a sudden hope and gladness, such as even her uncle's coming had not brought. And a great deal of her gladness and hopefulness was expressed in her tones as she held out both hands to him and said, "Dr. McHenry!"

23

THE DOCTORS AND THEIR PATIENT

His ways are not as our ways.

IT seemed to be a magic name, "Dr. McHenry"; little Dr. Jones drew himself up and bustled forward, and Mr. Nelson bent curious, searching eyes on the newcomer. The name was very well known in Lewiston, but Lewiston had never laid eyes on the great man before. "The five-hundred-dollar Boston doctor," he was jocosely called, by reason of the many fabulous stories that were afloat concerning his marvelous cures and equally marvelous prices; but fable aside, he was undoubtedly a wonderful doctor; and the joy in Dell's eyes did not compare with the feeling of sudden relief in her troubled heart. Dr. Jones was promptly introduced, and the question of brandy or no brandy again presented. "I can of course form no opinion until I see the patient," said the grave-voiced Boston doctor. So daughter, uncle, and physicians went to the patient's room, the two others remaining outside, eager for the conclusion of the whole matter. A rapid examination of the patient's pulse, a few brief, rapidly put questions, and Dr. McHenry fixed his grave, gray eyes on the little doctor's face and spoke in slow, deliberate tones:

"It seems to me that there is plenty of febrile action already. I see no occasion for increasing it."

"Of course not," eagerly and rapidly commenced the little doctor; "and in ordinary cases I should not advise it; but the excitement of the patient is such that I thought it better to allay it with a very little of what he craves."

"Suppose his diseased stomach should choose to crave a dose of arsenic; what then?"

Very low, very grave was the question, and the great, gray eyes were fixed thoughtfully on the little man.

Dr. Jones crimsoned and made haste to answer:

"Of course we wish your advice in the matter. I have felt the need of consultation myself—and if you think—and I have no doubt you are right, but, the excitement, my friend. I assure you he has been perfectly raving for liquor all day. How would you manage that?"

"I should not hope to allay it by feeding him brandy." Still the very low, very grave tones.

At this point the sick man aroused from his uneasy slumber and began his petition for a drop of something cooling and strengthening. Meantime the Boston doctor had withdrawn into the shadow, motioning his companion to do the same. Dell offered her earnest explanation why it was impossible to gratify him, to which he responded with impatient and contemptuous exclamations. Dr. Jones bustled up to him and offered his crumb of comfort:

"We have decided, Mr. Bronson, that the nervous condition of your system is such that we shall have to refuse you all liquors for the present."

"Nervous fiddlesticks!" said Mr. Bronson in feeble anger. "When did you decide it? Seems to me you've wonderfully changed your mind; you told me not an hour ago that it would do me good to have a drink."

"Not quite that, Mr. Bronson," replied Dr. Jones, with crimsoning face; "but since that time we have had a consultation and decided differently."

"Who has?"

"Dr. McHenry, of Boston."

Mr. Bronson knew the name very well indeed; for about half a minute he was awed and astonished; the next he clearly believed Dr. McHenry to be a myth, so far at least as his presence in Lewiston was concerned.

"I don't care for all the doctors in Boston put together," he said in utmost peevishness. "I want a drink of brandy, and I'm going to have it."

Dr. McHenry stepped quietly forward.

"Let me try," he said to Dr. Jones; then he stepped to the bedside, fixed those singular gray eyes of his on the patient, and spoke in clear, steady tones:

"My friend, are you entirely ready to die?"

A sudden shiver ran through Mr. Bronson's frame, and for once his attention was turned from brandy.

"Are *you*, Dr. McHenry?" he asked in an awed tone.

"I am," and then the doctor repeated his question, the steady eyes meantime reading the sick man's face.

Mr. Bronson's voice grew very husky and trembled over his next question:

"Am I going to die?"

"That is more than I can tell you; but I can state the case frankly. You have burnt up your stomach with rum; that is much worse to manage than the burns on your body and makes things more serious for you. At the same time, if you will aid us like a man in our efforts by trying to understand that whiskey, in all its forms, is your worst enemy, and if you will refuse to touch a drop, even if it is offered you; and will undertake the work of trying to keep your mind calm and quiet, we propose, with God's help, to see you safely through your trouble. But if you persist in fretting yourself into a fever over a poison which you must not have, or if anyone is so cruel as to bring you brandy, and you are so insane as to drink it, your life will not be worth that." A sudden emphatic snap of Dr. McHenry's thumb and finger gave point to this startling sentence; and the mind of Mr. Bronson was most effectually set at rest on the liquor question.

The days that followed were full of sickening anxiety. The patient had drained his constitution years before and had very little left with which to endure his pain; then there was added to his torment the burning of a perpetual craving thirst that refused to be allayed by anything that was within his call. Still Dr. McHenry's words had thoroughly sobered and frightened him, and he gave what help he could in trying to smother his longings and control his unsteady brain. As for Dell, her faith had returned to her; she did not let it go again for an instant. When her Uncle Edward told her gently, "Dear child, you must be prepared for the worst, Dr. McHenry thinks the case more than doubtful," she looked up in his face with a calm, brave smile and answered steadily:

"He will not die, Uncle Edward; God will not let him die until he is safe."

Firmly she clung to her belief. When on the fifth day he seemed to sink beyond all human aid; when in answer to a beseeching telegram, Dr. McHenry came again and, arriving late in the day, came on tiptoe to the bedside and stood with the rest awaiting in solemn silence the departure of a soul—even then Dell's face was calm and hopeful—she responded in person to Mr. Nelson's call, and in answer to his inquiry said:

"They think he is dying—but he is not. I *know* God will not let him die."

"I never saw one apparently so near death's door," Dr. McHenry said afterward. "I had no idea he would ever speak again."

"That was very powerful medicine that we administered," Dr. Jones said, rubbing his hands in satisfaction. And Dr. McHenry answered quietly:

"It was not medicine that called him back; it was the prayer of faith."

Gradually there dawned upon Dell a knowledge of what *"his* way" was to be—not after her shaping—yet God had given her in her inmost heart the assurance that her father should not die until that "thought" that he had "toward her," to give her "an expected end," was accomplished. It was for that purpose that she believed that the almost departed soul had been bidden to tarry for a little, long enough to hear and accept the pardon at the eleventh hour.

Not so; and gradually there came to her the knowledge that her share of the work was not yet done; that the father was to *live* indeed, that is, that no further immediate danger was to be apprehended; that his life might even, probably *would*, be lengthened out by years; that he would be crippled and deformed, needing her constant care and thought, needing to be watched over and fed and cared for like a child; and that there would be no childlike gentleness and submission and love to make the work pleasant and hopeful. As the weeks passed, the excitement and deep interest that had been awakened in the hearts of the people died quietly out.

The village was no longer put in a flutter over Dr.

McHenry's comings and goings; the great man had done his work for the poor cripple and came no more. Uncle Edward still came and went, spending one afternoon of every week with his child, strengthening her and helping her, and by means of his cultured taste and ample purse, gradually making the two rooms that they occupied at the Widow Parker's into bowers of beauty. Mr. Nelson and Jim Forbes and Sam Miller were patient, faithful, constant friends; yet still the weight of the work and the burden rested on Dell. And heavy the burden certainly seemed. Never in his most hopeless, liquor-drinking days had Mr. Bronson been more fully determined to hear not a single word of a religious nature. Indeed, his indifference seemed to have been changed into positive vindictiveness; he would not listen to a prayer from his brother-in-law; he would not allow Dell's Bible to be kept on the little stand at the foot of his bed; he stopped her harshly if she began what he called one of her "Psalm tunes," and in every way he seemed to have gone backward. In every way save one—his brain was entirely clear from liquor during these days. Dr. McHenry's final warning had been too plainly and solemnly worded for even him to disregard; but he seemed bent on having vengeance on his marvelous self-denial by being as miserable in himself as possible, and making all around him share his misery. Meantime, Dell was completely shut in from the outside world. No more churchgoing for her; her Sabbath school class passed quietly into Mr. Nelson's hands; not one of them now but were quite willing to become his pupils, if their doing so would be any sort of comfort to Miss Bronson. The temperance meetings still went on, but they did without Dell.

"It is a good thing," she said, half laughing, half

tremulously, to Mr. Nelson one evening, after he had been giving her an account of a successful meeting and the addition of two new members from her class. "It is a good thing to discover that the earth can turn on its axis without your help—especially when you have been imagining that you did a great deal of the pushing."

She stood with her uncle in the hall on the afternoon of a wintry day; he was drawing on his gloves, and buttoning his overcoat, and otherwise preparing for his snowy walk to the train. A whole week, perhaps two, before she would see his dear face again.

"Doesn't the little heart ever quail, just the least bit?" he said, looking down on her and holding her to him with a yearning father's tenderness. It had been an unusually hard afternoon; Mr. Bronson had been in his bitterest mood, and there had come over the heart of the Boston merchant such a dismal sense of contrast between the life his darling was living now and the shielded, carefully nurtured life that she had lived in her Boston home that he fairly longed to carry her back into the brightness.

She looked up wistfully. "No, Uncle Edward, at least not often; not when I lean on the 'Strong Arm' for strength. You are almost discouraged, I think, but I am not. Do you know I would rather have this intolerance of the whole subject than the absolute indifference that possessed him so long? I think almost any phase of the heart is better than indifference."

"You are right," he said quickly. "An angry conscience is an aroused conscience oftentimes. Well," as the train shrieked around the corner, "good-bye, dear child. God bless and keep you, and give you the desire of your heart. What are you specially resting upon today?"

She repeated it with an earnest, wistful light in her eyes: "His ways are not as our ways"; and her uncle added with hopeful tenderness, "His ways are always right."

She stood at the window and watched him as he sped down the snowy street, the man who had been to her in every respect a father. Only a moment did she give herself the luxury of looking after him with loving eyes; then she turned and went back to the waiting father inside, stilling her heart in the meantime with the thought that watching over and caring for them all was that other Father, whose daughter she really was.

24

⊷⊱✦⊰⊷

THE STRANGE WEDDING

*Great and marvelous are thy works, Lord God Almighty;
just and true are thy ways, thou King of saints.*

THE October day was aglow with beauty, all the leaves
of the trees had adorned themselves with spots of
scarlet and crimson and gold, and the leaf-strewn
earth rustled gaily as you trailed your garments along
the walk. Over all, the magnificent sun poured his
yellow glory. It was just that time of high carnival that
the world takes on before it spreads its gray and naked,
frostbitten arms abroad, proclaiming that winter is at
hand.

Dell had been out into all the beauty, drinking it in
and gathering great glowing bunches of leaves. She
had come in again and dropped herself on a low
ottoman, letting the leaves shower around her, while
she set herself about arranging them into many-col-
ored bouquets; the side door stood open, letting in the
breezy freshness of the afternoon; an open fire burned
in the grate to dry and sweeten the October air. Dell
was in her favorite dress of snowy white; it was late in
the season for white dresses, and Lewiston people
thought her very absurd; but Dell, who had ever been
hopelessly indifferent as to what people thought

about her garments, said that black dresses and winter would come soon enough, so every bright afternoon she robed herself in white, and compromised with the season by adding a dainty scarlet sack, that matched the leaves in her hair and in the vases all about her.

Very happy and bright looked Dell on this particular afternoon, a sweet and settled peace shining in her eyes. Not a day older seemed she than that first afternoon in August, more than two years ago. The room in which she sat accorded well with her appearance; bright and fresh and beautiful was everything about her; simple, of course, to be in keeping with the low ceiling and the old-fashioned doors and windows, but fairly alive with comfort and in exquisite taste. There was only one large piece of furniture in the room, and that, a chair, elegantly upholstered, looking soft and downy enough for a bed in itself, and in this chair, his gaily slippered feet resting on the cushioned footstool, his crimson-lined wrapper folded comfortably around him, rested Dell's father. On his face change was distinctly marked; indeed, you would hardly have imagined that that smoothly shaven, neatly, even elegantly, dressed old man could be the miserable, red-faced, half-drunken wretch who sat with his slouched hat pushed to one side and his feet tilted above his head on that memorable evening of the fire.

"Father," Dell said suddenly, holding up a bunch of the brightest leaves, "did you ever in your life see anything prettier than that?"

"Yes," he said slowly, in a fond, happy voice, looking beyond the leaves to the bright face back of them. "They're wonderful pretty, but I've seen something a great deal prettier—I know where." Dell laughed, a happy little laugh; the flattery, broad and absurd as it was, was very sweet to her hungry heart; and that man was her father. He watched her in pleased silence for a few minutes, then he said, "You may bring me the book if you will, child, and I'll read a bit," and Dell brought forward a light stand, so made that it would slip inside of the wheeled chair, and thereupon she placed the handsomely bound, large-print Bible; herself adjusting the glasses that the poor shriveled hands had not strength to arrange, and then went back to her work. She had, meantime, procured a large book for herself, and now gave her attention to the selection of the prettiest leaves for pressing, stealing occasional loving glances at the old man bending over The Book.

Great and marvelous indeed had been the changes wrought in that past year! *His ways* are wonderful indeed; through much suffering and many disappointments, after dark days of hope deferred, the "expected" end had come, and Dell beheld her father reading with reverent face, and eyes full of earnest interest, the Bible stories so new and precious to him. Life was very bright to Dell during these days; with the constant care and the constant prayer that she had bestowed on her father, there had come into her heart a great and overpowering love—stronger than any filial love that she had ever imagined, and during those later months with the love had come a feeling of reverence—almost of awe—as she felt the babe in Christ, springing into higher knowledge and stronger faith than she had attained. As she looked at him, she realized that every gray hair in that bent head was dearer to her than her own life. Looking at him and thinking of the changes, she went back a little over her own past; her efforts in the cause; her hopes and plans and disappointments and victories. "No," said Dell, with a puzzled face, after a moment's earnest thought,

"I have tried to work hard and accomplish a great many things, but I believe I have done none of them. Well, what difference does it make? Many of the very things I wanted have been done, and if the King has accepted my trying and done the work himself, what is it to me so long as the work is done?"

There were some things not yet done. There was Mr. Tresevant. Dell thought of him, but without a shade on her face; he would come into the light yet, she felt certain of it. The cloud still rested between them; he had never forgiven her for the slight that he still chose to think she had brought upon him at the time of Chester Elliot's funeral. She had never seen him alone for a moment since that time, and during his very rare calls on her father he had been only coldly polite to her; but Dell was forever looking forward to the day when he would understand everything in its true light. She did not know how it was to be brought about; perhaps some chance word of his would give her an opportunity to explain. *Some way,* she could not tell how, it would all come right. Meantime, she had lost all her hard, bitter feelings toward him; she had even come to the point of justifying his cruel suspicion of her, and spent much of her time in a sort of gleeful looking forward to the days wherein they, having come fully to understand each other, would talk over together these dark days of separation. About the main point that had separated them, she had not a doubt; the temperance question was taking on new force and power; with every passing day, new men—strong ones—were coming to the front to aid in the warfare. Mr. Tresevant was too good a man to remain long in the shadow; once convinced that he had done her injustice, he would be the first to frankly admit it; then, loving her entirely and heartily even as she did him, he would be led to look into the matter with all his heart and, looking at it thus from a Christian standpoint, would not fail to be convinced, and once convinced nothing would keep him from standing up firmly for the right. Thus reasoned Dell, and watched with every passing day for the time to come. She was always saying to herself, Perhaps this is the very day that is to set things right. She said it on this particular afternoon. *Perhaps he will be in to see Father, and then who knows what may happen? Someday I will frankly say to him, "You did me very great injustice that time; don't you know you did?' And then I shall explain it all to him. I am not sure but that would be the right, true way to do. I would have done it long ago if he had given me a chance. It was a good while ago, more than a year now. But he will not be in this afternoon—I remember now—he is in Boston, stopping with the Burtons. I wonder why they went to their town house so early this year? Poor Laura!* And then Dell drew a little sigh as she could not help doing when she thought of that fair, young widow—and how the brightness of her brief married life went out in such awful gloom.

Something about Laura made her think of Mr. Nelson, but she did not like to think of him during these days; a very sad thing had come to pass. It was nearly three weeks since he had called on her; it was after her father was made comfortable and at rest for the night; she had been so glad to see Mr. Nelson in their cozy parlor; she admired and liked him so much; she had shown her pleasure so frankly and joyously, but he had overwhelmed her. In all their free, glad meetings together, it had never occurred to her that he was looking forward to her hopefully as his wife. When he told her so, in his frank, hopeful way, it smote her heart with a great grief. In her carelessness she felt that she had led him astray; she made all the reparation in her power; she told him gently and humbly of her preoccupied heart; of a certain trouble that came between them darkening her future, but of her hope and belief that it would be cleared away; in short, she made him her confidante as she realized now that she ought to have done long before—her confidante, except that she spoke no name and gave no definite account of the trouble—but after a painful silence he had suddenly said:

"Is it Mr.—?" then as suddenly stopped and blushed to his very temples and added hastily:

"I beg your pardon. I have no right. I thank you, Dell, for your confidence; some other time I can talk with you; good-night," and he suddenly vanished. That was three weeks ago, and she had not seen him since. It seemed very hard that there must be just so many dark lives in this world. Just then occurred a break in her reverie. Tommy Truman called with the mail—the daily papers that Uncle Edward always sent. Tommy was in haste; no time for a chat, so Dell, her father being still absorbed in his reading, unfolded the crisp sheet and glanced down the column of daily news, skimming one item after another until suddenly her eyes were riveted. Twice she read over the familiar words:

"In Boston, October 23, at the residence of the bride's parents, by Rev. J. C. Holbrook, D.C., assisted by Rev. Chester Tremain, D.D., Rev. Carroll C. Tresevant, of Lewiston, to Mrs. Laura Elliot, only daughter of Robert Burton, of this city."

The paper lay very still in Dell's lap; she folded her hands above it and sat looking steadily into vacancy. Sat for she did not know how long; but when she roused again the sunlight had disappeared; thick leaden-colored clouds were over the sky. Some of her leaves had dropped near the grate, and the fire had withered them; they rustled and broke underneath her feet as she arose and trod on them; she took her little hearth broom and swept them all into the grate; they blazed up for a moment, and then smoldered and shriveled and died out. Dell shivered; the room was cold. She closed the door and added more coal to the grate.

"Dell, my child," said her father, looking up from his book, "do you remember the night that I got you to come into that room over there and sing for us wretches, and you sang a hymn?"

"Yes, Father, very well, indeed."

"Well, do you know, child, I really believe it was then that your old father began to think; you thought I was most asleep, but I wasn't, and you thought I went on from bad to worse after that, and maybe I did; but, for all that, you put words into my head that night that I never got rid of, day nor night afterward, drink as hard as I could, and the Lord used them very words to bring me to myself at last."

Dell came over without speaking a word and wound her arms around her father's neck, and laid her soft brown head against his gray one. He would never know what balmy words he had been speaking, nor how her sore heart needed them.

"Look here, child," he said, leaning forward again to "The Book." "I've found a verse for you and me. I'll read it, and you see if it ain't exactly so. I never came to that verse before." And in slow, tremulous tones he read:

"And I will bring the blind by a way they know not; I will lead them in paths that they have not known; I will make darkness light before them, and crooked things straight. These things will I do unto them, and not forsake them."

Dell drew a quick breath. "Yes, Father," she said, "it is for us." She had "come to" this verse before, but it had never so come to her. As she drew the shades and lighted the lamp and went about her father's tea and toast, she whispered it over and over: "I will make darkness light before them, and crooked things straight. These things will I do unto them, and not forsake them."

In a subsequent volume our readers will hear more of Dell.

THE END

Other Living Books Best-sellers

400 CREATIVE WAYS TO SAY I LOVE YOU by Alice Chapin. Perhaps the flame of love has almost died in your marriage, or you have a good marriage that just needs a little spark. Here is a book of creative, practical ideas for the woman who wants to show the man in her life that she cares. 07-0919-5

ANSWERS by Josh McDowell and Don Stewart. In a question-and-answer format, the authors tackle sixty-five of the most-asked questions about the Bible, God, Jesus Christ, miracles, other religions, and Creation. 07-0021-X

BUILDING YOUR SELF-IMAGE by Josh McDowell and Don Stewart. Here are practical answers to help you overcome your fears, anxieties, and lack of self-confidence. Learn how God's higher image of who you are can take root in your heart and mind. 07-1395-8

COME BEFORE WINTER AND SHARE MY HOPE by Charles R. Swindoll. A collection of brief vignettes offering hope and the assurance that adversity and despair are temporary setbacks we can overcome! 07-0477-0

DR. DOBSON ANSWERS YOUR QUESTIONS by Dr. James Dobson. In this convenient reference book, re-nowned author Dr. James Dobson addresses heartfelt concerns on many topics, including questions on marital relationships, infant care, child discipline, home man-agement, and others. 07-0580-7

THE EFFECTIVE FATHER by Gordon MacDonald. A practi-cal study of effective fatherhood based on biblical principles. 07-0669-2

FOR MEN ONLY edited by J. Allan Petersen. This book deals with topics of concern to every man: the business world, marriage, fathering, spiritual goals, and problems of living as a Christian in a secular world. 07-0892-X

FOR WOMEN ONLY by Evelyn R. and J. Allan Petersen. This balanced, entertaining, and diversified treatment covers all the aspects of womanhood. 07-0897-0

GIVERS, TAKERS, AND OTHER KINDS OF LOVERS by Josh McDowell and Paul Lewis. Bypassing generalities about love and sex, this book answers the basics: What-ever happened to sexual freedom? Do men respond differ-ently than women? Here are straight answers about God's plan for love and sexuality. 07-1031-2

Other Living Books Best-sellers

HINDS' FEET ON HIGH PLACES by Hannah Hurnard. A classic allegory of a journey toward faith that has sold more than a million copies! 07-1429-6 *Also on Tyndale Living Audio 15-7426-4*

HOW TO BE HAPPY THOUGH MARRIED by Tim LaHaye. A valuable resource that tells how to develop physical, mental, and spiritual harmony in marriage. 07-1499-7

JOHN, SON OF THUNDER by Ellen Gunderson Traylor. In this saga of adventure, romance, and discovery, travel with John—the disciple whom Jesus loved—down desert paths, through the courts of the Holy City, and to the foot of the cross as he leaves his luxury as a privileged son of Israel for the bitter hardship of his exile on Patmos. 07-1903-4

LET ME BE A WOMAN by Elisabeth Elliot. This best-selling author shares her observations and experiences of male-female relationships in a collection of insightful essays. 07-2162-4

LIFE IS TREMENDOUS! by Charlie "Tremendous" Jones. Believing that enthusiasm makes the difference, Jones shows how anyone can be happy, involved, relevant, productive, healthy, and secure in the midst of a high-pressure, commercialized society. 07-2184-5

MORE THAN A CARPENTER by Josh McDowell. A hard-hitting book for people who are skeptical about Jesus' deity, his resurrection, and his claim on their lives. 07-4552-3 *Also on Tyndale Living Audio 15-7427-2*

QUICK TO LISTEN, SLOW TO SPEAK by Robert E. Fisher. Families are shown how to express love to one another by developing better listening skills, finding ways to disagree without arguing, and using constructive criticism. 07-5111-6

REASONS by Josh McDowell and Don Stewart. In a convenient question-and-answer format, the authors address many of the commonly asked questions about the Bible and evolution. 07-5287-2

THE SECRET OF LOVING by Josh McDowell. McDowell explores the values and qualities that will help both the single and married reader to be the right person for someone else. He offers a fresh perspective for evaluating and improving the reader's love life. 07-5845-5

Other Living Books Best-sellers

THE STORY FROM THE BOOK. From Adam to Armageddon, this book captures the full sweep of the Bible's content in abridged, chronological form. Based on *The Book*, the best-selling, popular edition of *The Living Bible*. 07-6677-6

STRIKE THE ORIGINAL MATCH by Charles Swindoll. Swindoll draws on the best marriage survival guide—the Bible—and his 35 years of marriage to show couples how to survive, flex, grow, forgive, and keep romance alive in their marriage. 07-6445-5

THE STRONG-WILLED CHILD by Dr. James Dobson. Through these practical solutions and humorous anecdotes, parents will learn to discipline an assertive child without breaking his spirit and to overcome feelings of defeat or frustration. 07-5924-9 *Also on Tyndale Living Audio 15-7401 0*

SUCCESS! THE GLENN BLAND METHOD by Glenn Bland. The author shows how to set goals and make plans that really work. His ingredients of success include spiritual, financial, educational, and recreational balances. 07-6689-X

THROUGH GATES OF SPLENDOR by Elisabeth Elliot. This unforgettable story of five men who braved the Auca Indians has become one of the most famous missionary books of all time. 07-7151-6

TRANSFORMED TEMPERAMENTS by Tim LaHaye. An analysis of Abraham, Moses, Peter, and Paul, whose strengths and weaknesses were made effective when transformed by God. 07-7304-7

WHAT WIVES WISH THEIR HUSBANDS KNEW ABOUT WOMEN by Dr. James Dobson. A best-selling author brings us this vital book that speaks to the unique emotional needs and aspirations of today's woman. An immensely practical, interesting guide. 07-7896-0

WHAT'S IN A NAME? Linda Francis, John Hartzel, and Al Palmquist, Editors. This fascinating name dictionary features the literal meaning of hundreds of first names, character qualities implied by the names, and an applicable Scripture verse for each name. 07-7935-5

WHY YOU ACT THE WAY YOU DO by Tim LaHaye. Discover how your temperament affects your work, emotions, spiritual life, and relationships, and learn how to make improvements. 07-8212-7